THE GRAVE MAN

A SAM PRICHARD MYSTERY

THE GRAVE MAN

DAVID ARCHER

USA TODAY BESTSELLING AUTHOR

"...THE NEXT JACK REACHER!"

1

Going to the office wasn't as pleasant lately, Sam thought, as he made his way through the back entry to the detectives' division. There weren't so many people there that day, and it seemed like a lot of them were avoiding the place, just staying away as much as they could. He could understand that.

After almost ten years as a Denver cop, Sam was sick of seeing what humanity was really capable of. He had grown up reading cop stories, always seeing how the cops would save the day, watching them rescue the innocent and punish the guilty every week on TV, until he finally knew that he had to be one himself. After a short stint in the Army that never even got him out of the country, he'd come home and applied for the academy. He'd been accepted, and that was the start of an illustrious career.

Now, it was all he could do to drag himself out of bed in the mornings, make himself come in and see what new horrors he'd have to deal with. The past four months he'd been on loan to the DEA, and they'd made some big drug busts, shut down some of the most evil purveyors of sin and death that ever lived, but they were like the mythical hydra—as soon as you cut off one of its heads, three more grew back to take its place.

Sam wanted to stop cutting off heads and find the creature's heart, but there was almost no evidence as to where that heart might be. They knew there was something big behind the drug operations in the city, but it was so well organized and so carefully designed that no one seemed to have any idea where or how to find it.

His cell rang as he sat down at his desk, and he saw his partner's number. Dan Jacobs was already out on his station, watching one of the dealers they'd identified the day before.

"Yo," Sam answered.

"Sam, it's Dan. I been thinkin', and it seems to me that we might be lookin' in the wrong direction, y'know?"

Sam blinked a couple of times. "Danny, I've been awake for about fifteen minutes, and haven't even opened my Starbucks yet. What the heck are you talkin' about?"

"I'm sayin', maybe we're goin' about this all the wrong way, tryin' to find dealers and trail 'em, follow the tracks up the ladder. There's something about this whole setup that smacks of serious organization, something big enough to hide in plain sight, know what I mean? If it's that well laid out, we can follow minions all day long, we're never gonna find the top guy, because they don't ever see the top guys."

Sam nodded. "Yeah, you're probably right," he said, "but unless you got a crystal ball lead on where else to go, I don't know what good it's doin' us. Where else we gonna find any leads at all? Got a clue, there?"

"Maybe," Dan said. "We've been tailing a lot of these clowns the past few weeks, right? Have you noticed one thing they all do the same?"

Sam thought about it, but nothing jumped out at him. He looked at it from a couple of different angles, then shook his head. Into the phone, he said, "Nope. So, what is it?"

"Facebook. No matter what else they're doin', these bastards never miss checking in on Facebook every day, several times a day. They go on, look at what people are sayin' on their pages, sometimes they answer and sometimes they don't, and then they go back to their drug dealin' ways."

Sam rubbed his temple. "Dan, everyone does that. Everyone on freakin' earth is on Facebook, and always checkin' it out. That's just part of modern livin', old buddy!"

"I know, I know, but hear me out. The only time they ever go make a drop or get money is right after they're on Facebook. I think maybe the stuff that's being said on there is some sort of code or somethin', a way to let 'em know when and where, y'know?"

Sam's phone beeped. It was their boss, Agent

Carlson. "Dan, I got Carlson beepin' in, lemme call you back." He hit the button to switch calls before his partner could answer. "Prichard," he said.

"Sam, we got a hit on the north side crew; they got a big load in, overnight, and they're cuttin' it out today. I'm pulling everyone in, we're gonna take 'em down. Where's Dan at?"

"He's on a stakeout, watchin' Pink Dog and his crew. Want me to bring him along?"

"Yeah, get him. Meet us at the back of the AT&T Building downtown, by their freight entrance. We're staging there. Can you make it in twenty?"

Sam checked his phone, thinking about how no one bothered to use watches, anymore. "Yeah, we'll be there. Later."

He hung up and dialed Dan back, told him where to go, and hung up again, grabbing his coffee and rushing back out to his car. The AT&T Building was downtown, which meant the raid was going to be in a high-traffic area. That was never good, and Sam got that nagging feeling in the pit of his stomach that he often got when things were likely to go wrong. He'd never come to the point of thinking of it as a predictor, but he'd felt it before, when things went way out of control, so it made him nervous and cautious. If something bad was going to happen, he wanted to do everything in his power to make sure it didn't happen to him or his partner!

He made his way across town quickly, but without

turning on his Christmas lights. Whoever they were about to hit would certainly be listening to scanners and checking traffic reports, so any mention of a police car moving toward them with lights on would spook them. The idea in these cases was to avoid notice, catch them completely off guard, so that no one had any chance to destroy or tamper with evidence.

That was the big problem with drug raids, he thought. You never knew who on the inside of any gang might have connections on the force, and it wasn't uncommon for a cop to accidentally let slip something that gave them a tip-off. Even worse were the times when the perp was a cop's kin, and got a quick warning by cell phone minutes before a bust. That happened far more often than anyone wanted to admit; it wasn't that the cop involved was actually dirty, it was just a last-ditch attempt to get a nephew or cousin to walk away from the criminal life before it was too late.

Problem was, those phone calls and tips sometimes got officers killed. How could any cop live with that? Geez, how could any person live with it? Knowing you got a cop killed just to save someone from what would probably be nothing more than a slap on the wrist would be an awfully heavy load of guilt to bear.

Sam didn't have any nephews or cousins, and wouldn't tip one off anyway. His attitude was that if you made your bed, you had to lie in it, so if someone close to him got jammed up, that was their problem. Sure, if it was someone who might have a chance of coming out and going straight, he might stand up for them at sentencing, or something like that, but he'd never risk letting a perp know what was going down. He'd let his own mother get busted before he'd do that.

Good thing Mom wasn't into drugs, wasn't it?

Sam didn't have anyone he was that close to. His dad had died when he was a teenager, leaving a lot of weight on some young shoulders, but Sam had done his best to hold the rest of the family together. His mom was managing, working as a real estate agent for one of the better companies, but the market was slow, so she was lucky she was even earning a living. Now and then she'd get a little behind on some bills, and Sam would help out.

His sister Carrie was out in California somewhere, trying to become an actress. He didn't hear from her except maybe at Christmastime, and once in a blue moon when she also needed to borrow a few bucks. He always sent it, because that's what big brothers do, and what else did he have to spend any money on?

He'd been married, once, back when he was young and new on the force and thought a cop could have a family life. Jeanie was beautiful and sexy, and thought that the young cop who had pulled her over for a broken taillight was the hottest thing she'd ever seen, so she'd scribbled her phone number on the back of the warning ticket he gave her and handed it back to him. He'd called her the next day and they'd dated for four months, then married in a surprise elopement and bought a house through his mom two weeks later.

The house was awesome, with a big yard, a two-car garage and a decent-sized pool in the back. There were four bedrooms, for all the kids they planned to have, with one downstairs and three upstairs, and three bathrooms so no one would ever have to dance outside a bathroom door for too long. It was a wonderful house, and he looked forward to the day it would have kids running through it.

He was doing a lot of double shifts back then, saving up money so they could pay for the house they'd bought, and Jeanie said she understood and was proud of him. She lasted less than ten months before the long hours finally got to her, and he came home to find her packed and gone to her mother's house in Tampa, with a note explaining that she'd "sort of met someone." She filed for divorce, and since they hadn't had any kids yet and she didn't want anything from him, he didn't fight it. He kept the house, even though it was way too big for him all by himself, so he just lived on the first floor.

His only hobby was in his garage; during one case, a drug dealer was busted hauling a quarter-million bucks worth of meth and coke in a 1969 Corvette Stingray, and his vehicle was seized. The car was damaged during the bust, so Sam watched, and when it came up for auction, he bid on it and won, and was gradually rebuilding it. It was actually close to being finished, but Sam was always looking for one more thing to fix, afraid of not having even the car to occupy his lonely days when there was nothing left to do to it.

Okay, he told himself, *enough Memory Lane crap. Let's get back to reality!*

The AT&T Building was looming ahead, and he wheeled the big Dodge Charger squad car into the service and delivery driveway. He saw the staging ahead, with six DEA blackouts—the big black SUVs the agency used—and a SWAT van from the Denver PD. Parking out of the way, he got out and grabbed his vest and gear from the trunk before walking over to where Carlson stood.

"So what have we got?" he asked, and Carlson frowned up at him. His DEA boss stood about five foot eight, and was a classic case of "little man syndrome" if Sam had ever seen one.

"We've got about forty perps in a small warehouse, with somewhere between fifteen and twenty mil in pot and cocaine they're divvying up. Word is this is a new deal between some of the street gangs, that they're splitting up the city into territories and working together to run all the dope."

Sam shrugged. "Okay, so we take 'em down today, they'll be back with another load somewhere else tomorrow. Hell, half the assholes we arrest today will be back out before then, and workin' with the next new batch by morning."

Carlson leaned back and looked at him, as Dan

Jacobs walked up from his own car. "So you think we should just leave 'em alone and let 'em keep pushing this crap on the streets? The more we take away from them, the more they gotta spend to get it back. If we can hurt them economically, then we got a chance of slowing this stuff down, getting it off the streets and away from our kids."

"Hey, I'm not arguin', boss, you're preachin' to the choir! I just wish the courts would work with us, instead of against us! If we could keep some of these creeps locked up, that would slow the operations down, too."

Dan laughed. "Save it for the next election and run for office, why don't you? That's the only way you'll ever get that song and dance out there."

Sam glared at him. "Excuse me, sir, I ain't no politician! I prefer to be honest and work for my livin'!"

Carlson growled, "Okay, knock off the funnies. Let's group up. You guys will be with Matheny's group, going in the front door. The others will be crashing the back and side doors, and SWAT's here to back us up if needed." He led the way to where the rest of the agents and officers were standing around, already geared up. "All right, we're about to go. Remember, we don't want any grandstanding. This is a sweep, plain and simple; we're going in to round 'em up and take their goodies, and that's it. No heroics, and hopefully they won't be trying any, either! Everyone ready?"

There was an answering chorus of "*Hoo-Rah!*" and

Sam fought back the urge to laugh; not one of these guys had ever been a Marine, he was sure, but they did love to play tough. He nudged Dan, beside him.

"I'm so glad I've got you on my flank," he said softly. "I wouldn't trust one of those yahoos with my dog's life, and I ain't even got a dog."

"Yeah, well, you just remember that while I've got your back, you're the yahoo who's got mine! Let's get both of us in there and out alive, deal?"

"Deal!" Sam said, and they bumped elbows as they got into the back of one of the blackouts.

The trucks bounced them around as they pulled out of the lot, and Sam thought of the way they showed scenes like this in movies, with special vehicles where cops who looked more like soldiers were lined along the wall of something like a Hummer, with special armor and helmets protecting them, and weapons that looked like something from the future bristling everywhere. He stifled a laugh, fighting it down from that nervousness in his gut. Last thing he needed at that moment was someone thinking he was losing it.

When the action began, it was all at once. The trucks slid to a stop, each at its pre-designated spot, and the men and women inside poured out. They ran to position at the door, four on each side, as the ram slammed into the doorknob and bashed it open, and then all of them were inside, weapons ready, screaming, "Federal Agents, get on the ground!"

The building was an open warehouse design, with only a few pillars holding up the ceiling, and they could all see the activity going on out on the floor. There were several tables set up, and multiple piles of bricks of marijuana and bags of white powder. Each table held a mix of the two, and the mixes were being plastic-wrapped together into big bundles. The people working looked up as the cops and agents entered, but not one of them made a move to duck until more cops came pouring in through other doors, all screaming the same things.

Suddenly, all hell broke loose, as half a dozen of the workers reached for handguns and began firing wildly around at any of the cops they could see. There was the staccato rattle of automatic weapons fire, and instantly, everything seemed to go into slow motion for Sam. He saw one of the officers he'd worked with go down with a bullet to his head, and the shooter who got him took a dozen rounds that turned him into hamburger. Another shooter fired off several shots, and another cop went down, a woman, the left side of her face apparently gone, and Sam thought about the three kids she was so proud of, but there wasn't any time for that, so he turned to the shooter and blew him away.

Dan let out a strangled scream and Sam spun to see why; his partner was down, holding his side. The shooter had come from behind them, and Sam fired without even thinking as the guy aimed at Dan again and readied another squeeze on the trigger. The shooter went down in a spray of blood and brains, and Sam started toward Dan, but then a semi-truck slammed into him and he was thrown down onto the concrete floor, his head hitting it hard. He was stunned, and the noises around him seemed muffled, suddenly, like he had ducked underwater.

He knew it hadn't been a truck that got him; he knew it was bullets, and probably several of them. He was hit, and while all he could feel was a dull ache at the moment, he knew it was probably bad, and so he decided to take as many of these assholes with him as he could, just to even out the score. He rolled over to find a target, but everything was already over, and all the remaining perps were down with their hands on their heads. There were four of them over to the side, obviously dead, and he saw people working on his comrades who'd gone down.

Johnson, that was the name of the woman, and he saw enough to know that she wasn't dead. She was holding something against her own face, so maybe the wound was only bloody, and not as deadly as it had looked. One of the male officers who'd gone down had been covered by a jacket, his face no longer visible at all, so Sam knew he was gone. He wasn't sure who it was, and that made him wonder if anyone knew he and Dan had been hit.

Dan—he rolled back to find his partner, and saw him lying there not five feet away. He was alive, and even threw a smile at Sam, but it took a second to register what he was saying.

"...we got 'em, Sam, we got 'em, we got the bastards who got us! I shot yours, and you got mine, ain't that cool?"

Sam managed a smile and gave a thumbs up, but he couldn't get his head to work well enough to speak. He tried to raise it and look around, but something big and dark fell over him, and everything was gone.

* * * * *

When the lights came up again, Sam thought he must have died, because this much white must have been Heaven. He'd always known he was good with the Lord, ever since that church camp when he was twelve, and even though he'd made a few mistakes along the way, he was still sure of his ticket to the Pearly Gates. He was glad he'd never let himself get like so many others who tossed it off, pretended they cared about God but didn't really even believe in him. Sam believed. He'd held on to that faith, and now that he'd bought the farm, here he was, in what had to be Heaven, because no place on Earth could ever look so clean!

A nurse walked in and saw that he was awake, and the whole fantasy of Heaven popped like a bubble. "Aw, crap," he said, and the nurse raised her eyebrows.

"Excuse me?" she asked.

Sam shook his head. "Sorry about that," he said, "it had nothing to do with you. It was just I thought for a minute I'd got killed and gone to Heaven, and I was kinda enjoying the idea. Then you came in and I realized I was still alive and stuck in this mess."

The nurse scowled. "Well, forgive me for ruining your day, Mr. Prichard, but it's good to see you awake, anyhow. The doctor wanted to know as soon as you woke up, so I'll go call him now." She turned and flounced out the door.

"'Bout damn time you woke up," he heard from over to his left, and he looked over to see Dan there in another bed. "I been layin' here a day and a half waitin' for you to decide if you was gonna live or not. Glad you decided to stick it out!"

Sam smiled at his partner, and felt a sharp pain in his right hip as he rolled his head to look closer at him. "Ow," he said, and then again, "Ow! How bad you get hit, Danny?"

"Not terrible, just took one in the side that didn't even manage to hit anything important. Hurts like hell, though."

Sam looked at the bracelet on his right wrist, but it said nothing about what might be wrong with him. He felt his hip, and realized that there was an awful lot of gauze there, and it was terribly numb. "What happened to me?" he asked, but Dan shrugged his shoulders.

"I dunno," he said. "Docs won't tell me squat, on account of you never makin' an honest woman outta me."

Sam's eyes narrowed. "What?"

14

"Because we ain't married, or otherwise related, the docs say I got no right to know how bad you got hit, and wouldn't tell me zilch. I tried to explain that your partner is closer than a wife, but they didn't buy it."

"Good," Sam said, "I don't buy that crap either. If you were closer than a wife, you'd be over doin' my dishes."

"Well, well, Mr. Prichard," came another voice, and Sam turned to see a doctor walk in. "How are you feeling today?"

"I ain't worth a crap!" Sam answered. "I'm tryin' to find out how bad a shape I'm in, so if you're not the guy who can tell me, go find him, okay?"

The doctor smiled. "I'm Doctor Schmidt, and I'm definitely the guy," he said, "so relax and stop picking on my nurses." He picked up a clipboard that was hanging on the foot of the bed and glanced through the top couple of pages.

Sam shifted his position, and said, "Ow!" The doctor looked up and smiled.

"Well, that tells me that you know where you got shot, anyway. Your right hip was hit three times, all of them deflected down into it from your bulletproof vest. The right acetabulum, the socket that your thighbone's ball end fits into, was shattered, and we had to go in and basically put it all back together with several tubes of superglue and a handful of screws. You're going to be in a wheelchair for a while, because the glue and screws we put in won't stand up to a lot of walking around, and we don't want to put a cast on you at this point."

Sam was stunned. "A wheelchair? A *wheelchair?* What kinda cop you know goes around in a wheelchair? How long will I be outta work, Doc?" The doctor suddenly looked uncomfortable, and Sam sensed what was coming. "What?" he demanded. "What is it you ain't told me yet?"

"Mr. Prichard," Doctor Schmidt began, "what you need to understand is that this is something that is beyond any degree of medical skill to repair..."

Sam held up a hand to stop him. "Just hold it," he said, "just hold it. I get the feeling you're about to say something I don't wanna hear, and I want to take a minute and get myself ready, okay? You here with me, Danny?"

"Right here, Sam, I'm right here."

Sam closed his eyes tightly for a couple of seconds, and then forced himself to take a deep breath and relax. He opened his eyes again and looked at Doctor Schmidt.

"Okay, go ahead, then," he said.

Doctor Schmidt looked at him for a long moment, then sighed. "Mr. Prichard, the degree of damage to your acetabulum means that you will never walk normally again. Your right hip will have very limited range of motion, and simple things like normal running and jogging will be impossible to you. You will have difficulty with stairs, and will find ramps easier to handle. You will almost certainly need a cane a good part of the time, and that's even after physical therapy that will probably take a year or more. I'm afraid there is no possibility that you'll ever be able to return to active police work."

Sam lay there for a long moment without saying a word, then turned to look at Dan Jacobs. "You hear this crap?" he asked, and Dan nodded.

"I heard it, Sammy."

The two old friends looked at one another for a long time, and then Sam closed his eyes. The doctor left the room after a few moments more, and Dan lay there in silence, wondering how his friend was going to get through this one.

When morning came, Sam woke to find a whole new world being thrown at him. No sooner than breakfast was over, he was suddenly invaded by four people from HR, who had all kinds of forms for him to sign.

"What we're doing," said the guy in the fanciest suit, "is giving you full medical retirement, in accordance with the union's policies and procedures. That means that you'll get seventy-five percent of your current income for life, with bi-annual cost-of-living raises, and full medical coverage from now on, as well. We need you to understand that this is not disability income, and you may apply for state or federal disability income if you wish, but you would probably be denied because of your medical retirement income, so there isn't a lot of point."

The lone woman in the group shoved the suit aside and got right in Sam's face, which wouldn't have been such a bad thing under other circumstances, since she was cute. "Now, we also need you to understand that you have to comply with the instructions of your physician, and that any failure to comply, such as refusal of medications or treatments, refusal of surgery or physical therapy, and similar issues, can result in the loss of your medical retirement certification and income, including your medical insurance coverage and..."

The four of them droned on for quite a while, but Sam caught the gist of it. As long as he cooperated and did what the nice doctors wanted him to do, he'd get paid to stay home and take it easy. Since he couldn't be a cop anymore, that was fine with him; maybe he could finally get the Corvette out and drive it. It would be months before he was out of the wheelchair anyway.

The suits also told him that they were paying for a nice new powered wheelchair, and would have someone build a ramp at his house, leading up to his front porch. The doors and such were already wide enough, and since he only lived on the bottom floor, it was no big deal. He'd manage, and when he was inside and no one could see him, he and that wheelchair wouldn't need to be such buddies all the time, anyway; what the docs didn't know wouldn't hurt Sam, he figured.

The only bad part of all of this was that he could no

longer be a cop, which was all he'd ever wanted to be. He'd given most of his life to it in one way or another, even down to losing his wife over the job; if the truth were to be told, he didn't work the double shifts as much for the money as for the love of the job, so he could only blame himself for Jeanie finding another set of arms to roll around in.

Without being a cop, Sam Prichard wasn't really all that sure who he was. He was told that he'd have to go to a therapy group once a week, some deal about how to cope when you're no longer on the force, so he figured he could let his feelings out there, some. He knew some guys didn't like to talk at those shindigs, but he wasn't gonna be one of them. He was losing a big part of his identity, and he needed help to cope with that, so he would take advantage of whatever was offered.

He was released from the hospital a little more than a week after being admitted and rushed into surgery, and he was surprised when Dan Jacobs and Agent Carlson were the ones to show up and drive him home. Dan would be on desk duty for another week or so, but Carlson had not been hurt; Sam was actually glad to see the little butthole.

"You ready to stop pretending to be hurt and get off your lazy rear end?" Carlson asked.

"Ready as I'm gonna be, I guess. Good of you guys to come help the hospital toss me out on my ear!"

Dan grinned. "Yeah, isn't it? But then, what are

friends for?"

They helped him into the car, and drove him to his house. The new powered chair had been delivered there, and was waiting to be assembled in his garage, courtesy of his mom, who had met the truck there and opened the garage door so they could put it inside.

They opened the garage to get it out, but there was a hang-up. "The dang thing's still in the box, Ben," Dan said. "What good is that gonna do you?"

Carlson, surprising Sam once again, pointed to the big toolboxes that stood over by the Vette. "I bet there's instructions," he said. Sam and Dan looked at him like he'd grown a third ear. "What?" he shot back. "Look, maybe we're not Santa's elves, but we're not stupid, either! We can put it together, don't you think? What do you say, Jacobs, you in?"

Sam laughed at the look on Dan's face. "I'll tell you what," he said. "If you guys'll stick around and help me get Franken Wheelie all put together, I'll order in pizza and a twelve pack o' beer. Deal?"

The guys accepted his offer, and the beast was together and working an hour later. That prompted a goofy session in which they each took turns driving it around the garage and the yard. That ran down the not-yet-fully charged battery, so by the time they were ready to take it inside the house, they had to push it, and then Sam had to plug it into the wall and let it charge overnight. Luckily, there was an outlet right next to his couch, which is where he ended up sleeping.

He could walk short distances with a cane, but the docs insisted he do so as little as possible. They didn't have to say it too often, because it hurt like hell every time he tried, and since he'd be doing a lot of it during physical therapy, he thought he'd save that pain for those days. Still, it meant he could get to the bathroom without "the Monster," as he called the powered chair, and that was a good thing. Big mother wouldn't even fit through the bathroom door!

Once he was home, things began to settle in for him. He had some money put back, so he bought himself a used minivan, an old Chevy Astro, and had a ramp built into the back end of it so he could putt right inside and then get into the driver's seat and go wherever he needed to go. The ramp would fold down to let him get in and out, and fold up so he could close the doors and drive, so it was a pretty good setup. Of course, the only places he ever went were to physical therapy and group sessions, the grocery store, the parts store, and out to eat now and then.

After three months, the docs said he could give up the wheelchair and start walking around with the cane. It still hurt, but like they said, the pain was a sign that he was getting stronger and making improvement, so he parked the electric scooter in the garage and went to walking. He still liked the van, though; for some reason, sitting up higher in it was easier than getting in and out of a car would be, so he didn't trade it off like he'd planned.

At six months, he was starting to walk around a bit without the cane, and that's when he broke down and bought himself a motorcycle. His legs were strong enough to hold him up at stoplights, and it was something he'd always enjoyed but never felt he had time for, so this was his chance. It felt good, and he noticed that he was even being checked out by some girls now and then.

His bike wasn't a Harley, but that didn't seem to matter to the girls. His old Honda Shadow, a sort of "Harley wannabe," got some attention as he rode it around town, and now and then, he'd even get to talk to a girl at a stop light. Once, a girl pulled up beside him and said absolutely nothing, but hurriedly dug out a piece of paper and scribbled a number on it. She handed it to him, held her hand to her face as if it were a phone and mouthed the words, "Call me!" as she drove away.

You sure don't get that on a powered wheelchair, he said to himself. *Should have bought a motorcycle sooner!*

He tucked the number into his shirt pocket, and found it later that evening when he was getting ready to shower. He looked at the name, Judy, thinking about how long it had been since he'd even been on a date, then grabbed his phone and called.

"Hi," he said when a feminine voice answered. "Is this Judy? You gave me your number today, and this is the first chance I've had to give you a—yes, on the motorcycle, that was me, yeah. Well, I would have called sooner, but I've been pretty busy today. What do I do? Well, I, um, I'm a retired cop, but I'm still called in sometimes as a, as a consultant! When they have a big case, y'know, sometimes I get called in to give my opinion about certain parts of it. Why am I retired? Oh, that's because I got shot a while back, and they gave me a medical retirement. I've got a bad leg, so I can't run like you have to when you take the police physical and such. Yeah, it's rough, but I'm a survivor. Well, I was thinking that if you wanted to, we could maybe go for a ride this Saturday? I love to ride up into the mountains, just get some clear mountain air, y'know? You would? That'd be great, Judy! Sure, I can pick you up there! Ten AM, that's perfect! I'll see you then!"

Saturday morning saw Sam out on the bike a little before ten, spare helmet strapped onto the sissy bar, ready to go out with a woman for the first time in more than three years. He climbed on and rode to Judy's house, over on the west end of Aurora. She saw him ride up and came running out, wearing a nice light leather jacket and some of the tightest jeans he'd ever seen spray painted onto a woman.

"Hi, Judy," he said, and she rushed up and kissed him full on the mouth. "Oh," she said, "I have been going nuts waiting for you to get here! Do you know how long it's been since I was on a motorcycle? Oh, god, I think it's been at least five years, and that is just too long!

I've been dying to get back on one for so long!"

She climbed on, and they took off, riding up 225 until it hit I-70, then following the Interstate west into the foothills of the Rockies. They rode for about four hours, and stopped at Aspen for lunch, visiting the historic Woody Creek Tavern for their famous tilapia tacos. Sam was ready to sit and rest a bit, his hip giving him fits for spending so much time on the bike—he hadn't really ridden into the mountains before—but Judy was ready to go again as soon as lunch was over.

Sam stalled as long as he could, then forced himself to smile as he got the bike fired up again. When he got her back home and dropped her off, Judy invited him to come in and stay a while, but he begged off and said he'd call her the next day.

He never called her again.

Another woman he met on the bike was Kathy, a short blonde who said she was a little afraid of motorcycles, but that she did like to have a thrill, now and then. He made a date with her for one evening that weekend, and she nervously climbed on and clung to him for half an hour as he cruised her around the city. She laughed in his ear at how much fun it was, and when he offered to buy her dinner, she asked if they could just go to one of the outdoor eateries, so he chose the Appaloosa Grill, one of the more refined patio dining experiences in Denver. She sat and talked with him for a couple of hours, and Sam was actually beginning to think he might want to date her again. He said so, and that was when she told him that she really enjoyed the ride, but she just didn't feel a connection to him, that going out with him felt more like hanging out with a brother than going on a date. He smiled and told her he understood, and took her home as soon as he got the chance.

He came to the conclusion that motorcycle dates weren't all they were cracked up to be, and stopped paying a lot of attention to the girls who flirted when he was on two wheels.

Sam was settled into the life of the medically retired cop. He tinkered with his car, tinkered with his bike, watched a lot of TV and Netflix, and tried not to think too much or too often about what Dan was doing, or his old team. Dan had come by a few times, but nobody wants to hang out with the guy who has cancer, and being forced into retirement was like having the big C to cops who were still on active duty. Sam couldn't blame him for not coming by anymore. He'd even stopped calling, finally, and Sam was sort of glad. It was too hard to find things to talk about that weren't connected to the old days.

He'd given up on all of those past hopes and dreams. That was why it was such a shock when he got dragged back into cop work once again.

2

The big Honda thumped underneath him and made him feel alive, sometimes, and he knew that his neighbors all watched as he rode it in and out of his garage. Some of the women flirted a bit, but he'd let it be known that he didn't flirt with his neighbors' wives, and so they made sure it was all in fun, and always right in front of their husbands.

He knew most of the neighbors, lately, because when the news about his shooting had gotten out, a lot of them had come over to tell him that they appreciated his service, and to offer any help he might need. He'd swallowed his pride and thanked them, even though offers of help only reminded him that he might need it, now, and that hurt worse than anything.

After a while, though, it was nice to be able to wave hello and goodbye to neighbors who were more than just a face you recognized as someone on your street, or to stop and talk to someone while he was mowing his grass. The first time he'd heard mowers outside his own window and looked out to see two of his neighbors out there, one on a mower and another running a weed-eater along his fence and walkways, it had brought him to tears.

He'd gone out and told them how much he appreciated it, and pointed out that he'd been planning to hire someone to do it, but they told him that's what neighbors were for. That led to a talk about his Corvette, which led to Sam's mechanical skills helping one of them —Jim Mitchell—put new brakes on his wife's car. Before long, there was a neighborhood swap system going on, and Sam never worried about his lawn again.

Everyone in the neighborhood could do something that someone else would need at one time or another, and so it became a kind of "pay it forward" situation. When someone needed mechanical work, Sam was glad to help out with his tools and knowledge, and when he needed some electrical work done, he found that the guy three doors down was a professional electrician, and that's whose rear axle Sam had fixed two weeks earlier. What goes around comes around, they say, and it was certainly working that way for Sam and his neighbors.

It had been a year since the shooting. Sam had adjusted well, so well that he'd graduated from his emotional support group and been released from physical therapy. He still used the cane a lot, but he could manage to go without it at times, and he'd even had a few more dates lately, though still not any he'd want to ask out again. Life was looking up a bit, and he was feeling like everything was alright, sitting on his front porch and watching the neighbors go past on their ways to work or visits or church or wherever they might be going.

He saw the lady walking up the street from a block away but didn't know who she was, so when she turned into his driveway and walked toward him, he was a little surprised. She came right to the edge of the first step, and stopped there.

"Are you Mr. Sam?" she asked.

She was a small woman who appeared to be in her late forties, and the lines in her face said she'd had her share of grief and heartaches. He smiled and motioned for her to come on up and take the other chair.

"That's me," he said. "How can I help you?" He suspected that she might have a problem with her car, and he was always ready to help out his neighbors. The "swap thing," as he called it, had given him a lot of purpose, and he enjoyed it.

The lady came up and sat beside him, but she didn't say anything for a moment. When she did, she didn't look up at him, and spoke softly, like she was trying to say a prayer but was a little bit afraid someone would overhear it and be angry.

"My granddaughter, she's gone missing, and the police say they can't help me. They say there's too much other stuff they have to do, so they can't look for a missing little girl."

Sam knew what she was saying, even if she didn't. It

wasn't that the police weren't interested, it was that they simply did not have the manpower to devote to every case that came along. If the child had been missing for less than a day, they wouldn't even take a report; if she'd been missing more than three days, they would assume she was either a runaway or dead. That was just how things went, and some cops were so callous that they didn't even bother to try to explain.

"What's your name?" Sam asked.

"I'm Sandy Ward, and my granddaughter is Cassie Rice. She's only twelve, Mr. Sam, and she didn't come home the other day after she went to visit with her daddy. He says he dropped her off, but nobody saw him, and she never came home." She finally raised her eyes to meet his. "Mr. Donaldson, down there at the end of the block, he said you used to be a policeman, and maybe you'd know how to find her."

Sam felt his heart breaking for the lady, but the words that rose to his lips were only, "I wish I could help, Mrs. Ward." As soon as he said them, he regretted it, because he knew that she'd take it as a sign that he didn't care, either, and if there was one thing Sam had always cared about, it was kids, but what could he do? He wasn't a cop anymore; he didn't have any way to help her.

She nodded, and looked back down at the floor. "I didn't figure you could," she said, "but he said I should ask, so I thought I would. I mean, you never know, right? Maybe there'd be something you could do, or maybe you'd know somebody who could. I had to try, right?" She got to her feet, and started down the steps. "Thank you, anyhow," she said, and Sam could almost hear the tears trying to fall as she spoke.

"Mrs. Ward," he said, "please come back. Maybe there is something I can do."

Once again, as soon as the words left his lips he wanted to kick himself, but it was too late. When she turned around, there was that faint glimmer of hope in her face, and there was no way he could bring himself to destroy it. He motioned for her to take the other seat again, and she did so, her eyes wide.

"Mrs. Ward, I used to be a police detective, and I even worked the department that looks for missing kids for a while, so I know the basics of what to do. The problem is that I don't have all the connections I used to have, and so if I go looking for Cassie, it's not gonna be like having the real police looking for her, you understand? Now, there's a chance I can find her, but I can't make any promises; if you can accept that, then I'm willing to give it a try, okay?"

Mrs. Ward nodded her head. "Mr. Sam, I can accept that, because as it is right now, no one is willing to do anything. I know you can't make any guarantees, but I *can* guarantee that if no one goes looking at all, then there's no way she'll ever be found, am I right?"

Sam smiled. "You're right. So tell me all about Cassie

and how she came to be missing."

"Cassie lives with me, since her mama got messed up on meth a few years ago, and her daddy gets her on weekends, even though he's in a lot of trouble himself. He hasn't gone to prison yet, though, so he still gets his parental rights, even though my daughter got hers taken away for the same charges he's facing. That just isn't right, but oh well. Not anything I can do about that. Anyway, Allen, Cassie's daddy, he came over five days ago to pick her up, late like always, but she didn't come back home that night like she was supposed to. I called him that night and asked him where she was, and he started yellin' at me, said he dropped her off right when he was supposed to, and if I lost her that was my own fault." She sniffled. "Mr. Sam, I know down in my heart that he didn't bring her back, and I know he's done something with her, but I don't think she's dead. I think if she was dead, he'd have been long gone by then, cause he's a coward."

"Sounds about right," Sam said. "His name is Allen Rice?"

"Allen Rice, yes sir," she answered. "He doesn't have a job, but he's always got money, and it doesn't take a genius to figure that out, not in this day and age. Cassie's told me herself that he's made her take packages and give them to people in exchange for money, but the court says I still have to let him take her for a visit every other Saturday."

Sam took out his phone and dialed a number from memory. "Dan? Listen, it's Sam."

"Hey, Sam," Dan said with a genuine smile in his voice. "Been a long time since you called, you doin' all right?"

Sam grinned. "Yeah, long time, that's true, and I'm doin' fair. Listen, Danny, I've got a small favor to ask, okay? You ever hear of a dealer, probably small time, name of Allen Rice?"

"Hmm, lemme see. What else you got on him? White or black?"

Sam covered the phone and turned to Mrs. Ward. "Allen's a white guy, right?" She nodded and he spoke into the phone again. "Yeah, Caucasian, probably early thirties or thereabouts. Might be known to use his daughter as a delivery mule."

"Hmm. I've got one Allen Rice in the database, and he's noted as using a little girl for parcel post. Lives on Princeton Drive, down in old town. Want me to see what else I can dig up on him?"

"Yeah, that sounds like my guy, so please do. The little girl's gone missing, and the grandma's a friend of mine, thought I'd see what I can dig up. I might call again if I need more info, is that okay? I don't wanna get you in trouble..."

"What trouble?" Dan asked. "I can talk to my old partner all I want to, and anyone don't like it can kiss my patootie!"

Sam laughed. "Okay, thanks man, you know I appreciate it! Later!"

He hung up the phone and turned to Mrs. Ward. "Okay, that was my old partner, and drugs is where we worked together. He knows Allen, and he'll get me some info on him. Meanwhile, can you get me a picture of Cassie, one I can hold onto?"

Mrs. Ward reached into a pocket of her jeans and took out a photo that she handed to him. "This is her," she said. "This was only taken a couple of weeks ago."

Sam took it, and saw a pretty little girl who was just at the stage of turning into a young adult. Cassie had honey-blonde hair and bright blue eyes, and the bare beginnings of a figure that would probably be driving boys crazy within a year. He tapped the picture on his hand and smiled at Mrs. Ward.

"Give me a day or so, and let me see if I can find anything. What's your number?" She gave it to him, and he put it into his phone to save it.

When she'd gone, Sam sat there for a long moment and thought about what he'd just agreed to do. With Dan's help, it was possible he could actually find out something about the child, but there were no guarantees. What if the worst-case scenario was true, and the child really was dead? There was no way to predict anything in police work, but he'd said he would try, so try he would.

His phone rang again a few minutes later, and he answered it instantly.

"Yeah?" he growled.

"Sam, it's Dan. I ran this guy through everything we got up here, and I may have something for you, if you can figure out how to use it. Remember I used to gripe all the time that some of these drug dealers were using Facebook? Well, there's a whole new website out there, and on the surface it's nothing, but there's a back end to it that seems to be how these guys are making their deals without leaving a trace. They're moving money in so many different ways that it's mind-boggling, too, and never leaving us anything to grab onto. We get little bits and pieces, but never any real info we can use to go after any of 'em, or shut 'em down."

"Wow," Sam said. "Sounds rough, but what's that got to do with my guy?"

"Well, it's a big 'if,' but if you can find a way into that network, you might find out what he's up to. From everything I can find, he's one of their people, working through this online network to sell his dope. Then all he does is drop it off, and he's done. The beauty of it is that even if we catch him, it's never with enough to make a difference; he's only got a small amount, and we can't even make a charge of 'possession with intent to deliver' stick. He never collects any money, so we can't get him for delivery of a controlled substance for sale, either. It's a nightmare."

Sam thought about it for a moment. "What's the website?" Dan gave him the name, drugspot dot org, and he memorized it so he could look it up later. "Thanks, Buddy, I owe you one. Keep your ears open on the little girl, too, okay? Cassie Rice is her name. Anything you hear, I wanna hear."

"You got it. You goin' into the private eye biz?" Dan asked.

Sam laughed. "No," he said, and then thought about it. "Well—maybe."

"Could be a good thing," Dan said. "Just remember that if you go into it as a pro, then that makes me your consultant, and I get a fee! Deal?"

Sam laughed out loud. "You got it, Bud! Talk to you later!"

Sam was decent with a computer, and had a nice one all set up in his dining room, but he wasn't a hacker. He played around on the dealers' website for a couple of hours, but all he saw was a bunch of pages about prescription drugs, how they work, what their side effects were, and things along those lines. He began to think that maybe he should try to find someone who could do what he and law enforcement couldn't: get into the back door of this site, even if it wasn't quite legally.

He went to craigslist and posted an ad in Computer Gigs:

Wanted: Someone who can wear a Dragon Tattoo. If you know what that means, answer by email asap!

The reference was to the book *The Girl With The Dragon Tattoo*, of course, which was about a girl who was a computer hacker. Sam had heard an arrestee use that term once, about someone who had hacked into police computer networks: "that dude could wear a dragon tattoo!" Now, Sam needed someone who could fit that description.

He waited about three hours, but there was no response. It was getting close to dinnertime, and since he'd forgotten to set anything out, Sam thought he'd just go out to eat. Taco Bell tickled his fancy now and then, and the weather was nice, so he climbed onto the Shadow and road off to the nearest one, out near the Mall. He liked the outdoor tables there, and often went through the drive-through to place his order, then rode around and parked so he could eat at one of them. That's what he did that day.

He'd gotten his usual—five regular tacos and a coke—and sat down at his favorite table, when his phone chirped to tell him he had a text message. He checked it automatically, and then read it again, his food all but forgotten.

Why does an ex-cop on medical retirement want a hacker? ~*Indie*

Sam thought fast. Whoever this was had managed to get through the craigslist email redirect and find out his real name, then dug into his past and learned an awful lot in a short time. This was either a trap of some kind, or exactly the person he needed. He typed:

Working on a missing child case privately. Need

some mad skills to help learn her fate.

He hit the send button, and then remembered the tacos. He ate while waiting to see if there would be another reply.

The phone chirped again, and he snatched it off the table.

We can talk. Are those tacos good? Buy me some?
~Indie

He was still squinting at the phone when the chair opposite was pulled out and someone sat down. He looked up and saw a short, pretty girl in her early twenties smiling back at him, phone in hand and a thick laptop case slung over her shoulder. She was around five feet tall, and her hair was multi-colored, dark underneath, but blonde on top. Combined with her big brown eyes, it was a strikingly pretty look, and when he let himself think it over, he changed that opinion from pretty to beautiful.

"I'm Indie," she said.

Sam looked at her for a long moment, then glanced down at his phone and back to her face. "I gather you're hungry?"

"Starving. I hope you don't mind I asked, but I was watching you eat and it got to me. I'd get my own, but I'm sorta broke at the moment."

Sam reached into his pocket and pulled out some bills, chose a twenty and handed it to her. "Here. You've earned that just by showing up here. Go get your food and then tell me how you did that."

Indie smiled and set her bag down next to Sam's chair, then hurried inside to order. She was back in four minutes, and sat down across from him again as he finished eating his last taco. She had four of her own and two burritos, with a large coke to wash it all down, and began eating furiously.

"I saw your ad, and sent a fake email to it with no data, but a packet that sent me a reply and then deleted the reply from your email client. That gave me your personal email address, so then I could Google you and get your name, which let me go digging for more info. I found where you got shot and lost your job as a cop, and that got me interested, so I looked deeper. I found your address and went and was gonna park down the road to watch you for a little bit, but then I saw you ride out, so I followed. When you started eating, I was hooked. So, what do you need a hacker for?"

Sam studied her for a moment. "Not so fast. If you're that good, why are you broke? I thought hackers were always loaded with money."

"Black hats are the ones who go after money. They're crooks. I'm not one of those. I'm more a gray hat; I'll do what I've gotta do to get done what I gotta get done, but I don't steal and I don't do this stuff for personal gain."

"Hmph," Sam said. "How do you make a living, then?"

She looked at him as if he were an idiot. "I get a job, like everyone else. Just happens I haven't been able to find one lately. Ran outta money last night, and I'll be outta gas soon. Is this a paying gig? If it is, and you're really out to help a kid, then I'm in."

Sam smiled. "It's a paying gig, and I'm really looking for a missing kid. Where do you live?"

The girl shrugged her shoulders. "Depends. Lost my apartment a couple months ago, so I've been doing the shelters. I'm supposed to go back to St. Mary's tonight. If I have to, if you need me close by or something, I can sleep in my car." She pointed to an older Ford Taurus in the parking lot.

Sam sat there and thought for a moment. "What's your name?" he asked.

She looked at him oddly again. "Indie, I told you. That's my real name, or sort of; it's Indiana, Indiana Perkins. My mom named me after Indiana Jones, cause she said it shoulda been a girl's name. Mom was stoned a lot, when I was growing up."

Without taking his eyes off her, Sam pulled out his phone and called Dan Jacobs again. "Dan, it's Sam again."

"No kidding," Dan said. "I'd never recognize your number!"

"Smart ass. You still at work?"

"When am I not? What do you need, Bud?"

"Tell me what you can find on a girl, Indiana

Perkins, early twenties, five foot nothin', blonde and brown."

"Gimme five," Dan said, and the line went silent.

Indie was smiling at him. "Holy Geez, you're checking me out? You do realize that you won't find anything I don't want you to find, right?"

Sam smiled back. "So tell me what we're gonna find," he said.

She shrugged again. "I went to MIT for IT, got a Bachelor's Degree, and been looking for a decent job for a year, now. No arrests ever, never been in any kind of trouble, and don't ever wanna be. That enough, or you want my shoe size?"

Sam grinned. "That'll do. Let's see if my partner can match it. You get enough to eat?"

She nodded. "Yeah. I'm gonna save the rest for later. Oh, here's your change!" She dug into a pocket and came out with the money.

"Keep it," Sam said, waving it away. "You said you need gas, right?"

Indie smiled. "Thanks, man. Really." She stuffed it back into her pocket.

Sam heard the phone come to life again. "Sam, still there?"

"I'm here, whatcha got?"

"Your girl is Indiana Marie Perkins, twenty-two, born in Eau Claire, Wisconsin, but moved here to Denver with her mother when she was about ten. She did well in school, got a degree in Information Technology from MIT of all places, then came back here and went to work for Dairy Queen for a while. Guess it didn't work out; she's had a few little jobs since then, but nothing steady, and nothing in computers. Looks like she's a single mom, got a little girl of her own, no father around. No wants or warrants, she's clean as a whistle, but there's a note that she might be homeless and if she's seen, then we're supposed to notify Child Protection Services."

"Thanks, Dan," Sam said. "I appreciate it. She might be a help on this thing I'm working on, just wanted to be sure who I'm dealing with. Catch you later."

"Okay. And by the way, I'm lookin' at her driver's license photo—she's kinda cute. Go get 'em, tiger!"

Sam hung up and looked at Indie. "Okay, you were mostly right. The only thing you missed is that he found out about your little girl. Where's she at?"

Indie seemed to crumple in the chair. "I was kinda hopin' they wouldn't mention that," she said. "She's actually asleep, over in the car."

Sam nodded. "So you were saving the extra food for her, right?"

The girl sat there and said nothing for a moment, then a tear spilled out of one eye. "Look, it's not easy taking care of a kid when you can't even find a decent job, okay? I do the best I can, but sometimes—I won't say I haven't thought about how easy it'd be to jack someone's credit, y'know, get money the easy way, but I never have done that, not yet, anyway. With the food and the money you gave me, we can get through another day, and if you're really gonna pay on this gig, then maybe I can make it another week or so. C'mon, man, don't turn me in, please? All I want is to work and take care of my kid."

Sam sat another moment and thought through what he was about to do, just trying to be sure it was what he wanted to do. He'd come to like his privacy, and he was about to throw it away.

"Here's the deal. I need your help, and you need a place to live. I've got a huge house with three extra bedrooms upstairs that have never even been used, and you've got a little girl you're gonna lose if the state finds out you're homeless. I think maybe we can solve each other's problem. Don't you?"

Indie looked at him for a long moment. "I've had offers like this before, man. I'll admit I'm pretty desperate, and you're not exactly ugly, but I'm not into anything really weird, got that? So, I mean, as long as you don't want anything kinky, then—well, maybe..."

Sam's eyes went wide and he held up both hands to stop her. "Whoa, whoa, whoa! You're reading me all wrong, Indie! No strings attached, not anything like that! All I want is your help with this case I'm on, and if you want to stay after that, then we can talk about rent, or helping out around the place, something along those lines! I'm not the kind of guy to try to take advantage of a girl in a bad situation!"

The two of them played stare-down for a minute, but finally Indie blinked. "Seriously? No strings? Just a place to stay while we work on this together?"

Sam nodded. "I'll provide the room and board, and pay you on top for whatever your work is worth, you tell me. But let's get you and your baby off the street, okay?"

Indie smiled again. "She's not exactly a baby, she's almost four. Her name is Mackenzie—Kenzie for short—and I'll warn you, she's likely to be all over you. She's never had a father and tends to grab onto men, if they let her. Is that a problem?"

"Nah," Sam said, shaking his head. "I like kids. And I've got a big TV in the living room, so she'll probably like that. The upstairs bedrooms—I set one up as a guest room, but the other two were supposed to be for kids eventually, back when I was married. There's not anything in them as far as furniture, so you and the little one will have to bunk together. I haven't been upstairs in probably two years, so I have no idea how dusty things might be up there."

Indie cocked her head to one side, and just looked at Sam. "You're an odd man, Samuel Prichard. Um—are we maybe talking about starting this tonight?"

"Yes," Sam laughed, "just follow me on home—oh, wait, you know where I live, don't you? Is there anything you need, for you or the little girl? I'm not sure what I'd have for food she might like, so maybe we should get some stuff." He reached back into his pocket and pulled out another pair of twenties. "Tell you what, take this and go by a grocery store, get whatever you think you'll need for the next couple of days, and meet me at the house when you're done. We'll go over the case, and go from there. Deal?"

The girl looked at the money in his hands, but made no move to take it. "I'm very good at what I do," she said. "If there's a way I can help you find this missing kid, I will. But this—what you're doing for me right now—I'll pay you back, somehow, on top of that." She took the money and then shook his hand. "Deal."

Sam watched her go back to her car, and saw her lean into the back seat with some of the remaining food. A little blonde head came into view for a moment, and then he saw the little girl's face light up when she saw food. Apparently burritos were high on her list of things she liked to eat, and Indie had bought her two of them. The child must have been hungry, too, Sam thought, because they were gone in what seemed like only seconds, and Indie handed over the coke before she got behind the wheel.

He could hear her telling the little girl that they had met a nice man who was going to let them stay at his house for a few nights, so they didn't have to go back to the shelter, and that they had to be very nice and not make a lot of noise, and other things parents say to kids when they feel like a burden has been lifted off their backs and they want the kid to be grateful.

Sam waited until she'd driven away before he got on the bike and rode home.

3

Indie drove up a half hour after Sam got home, and he held the door open as she carried in three grocery bags and a couple of small suitcases. The little girl, Mackenzie, followed her mommy and looked up at him with big, blue eyes.

"Kenzie," Indie said, "this is Mr. Prichard..."

"Just Sam," he said with a smile. "Mr. Prichard was my dad, and he's been gone a long time."

Indie grinned. "Okay, this is Sam. Can you say hi?"

The little one blushed and softly said, "Hi, Sam," then hurried after her mom into the kitchen. Indie said, "I got cereal and milk, and some peanut butter and jelly and bread and stuff like that. Oh, and I hope it's okay, I got some cookies and chips and stuff, too."

"That's fine," Sam said. "When you get it all put away, go upstairs and check out the guest room. I think the bed is all made up, but like I said, I haven't been up there in a couple years, so it may need some cleaning up. Then come on down and we'll find something on TV for

Mackenzie, and you and I can talk."

Indie smiled. "Okay," she said, and a moment later, she and her daughter went up the stairs to explore, with Indie dragging their two suitcases.

The second floor of the house was typical of suburban homes, with three bedrooms and a big bathroom. Indie and Kenzie looked through all of them, though only the first bedroom at the front of the house had been set up. There was a queen-size bed, a dresser and two nightstands; the furniture was from the sixties and looked like it might have come from a garage sale, but Indie wasn't about to complain. She checked the bed and found that while the covers were a little dusty, the sheets and pillows were clean enough. Fluffing the quilt got rid of most of the dust, or at least spread it out so it wasn't so visible.

She set their suitcases on top of the big dresser and opened them, then got Kenzie a pair of pajamas out. It was late enough that she hoped the child would be asleep soon, and wanted to get her ready. She set her up on the bed and began getting her changed.

"Tomorrow, we'll get you a bath," she said, "but you'll be okay for tonight. Let's just get you into your jammies, so you can be comfy, okay, babe?"

Kenzie looked up at her. "Is this our room tonight? The whole room?"

Indie nodded, smiling. "Yep, Baby, we get the whole room to ourselves, tonight. Nice, huh?"

"Uh-*huh*!"

The bathroom was dirtier, with thick dust on every smooth surface, and she noticed that the toilet bowl was completely dry. She flushed it, and was surprised to see rusty-looking water come flooding into the bowl, then realized that it had sat there so long unused that the water in the bowl had simply evaporated. She turned on the water in the sink and tub and let them run for a few moments, until the rusty color was gone and the water was clear, like it should be.

Indie decided she'd clean the bathroom up later, after talking to Sam. She wanted to find out more about the job he was offering her, and do her best to help find the girl who was missing, but at the same time, she wanted to know more about Sam, too. Not too many single men would let her and her daughter stay with them unless there were ulterior motives, but she thought he was being sincere when he said there would be no strings of that nature. Maybe there were some decent guys left, after all.

She gathered up her daughter and went back down the stairs.

Sam had gone to the living room and sat in his favorite recliner, just waiting for the two girls to come back down. Part of him wondered if he was nuts, letting them stay there, but he was pretty sure he could trust Indie. There was something about her that just said she was a good person in a bad situation.

He wondered if there were more to that situation than what he could see on the surface. Was it really that hard for a young woman to get a job? The little girl was old enough that she must have been born not long after Indie got out of high school; he wondered how she'd managed to go to college with a child, and whether anyone had helped her out.

Those things weren't any of his business, of course, but a cop's curiosity was always running wild. He'd have to try to keep it in check, at least where Miss Indie was concerned.

He heard voices a few moments later, and the girls came into the living room. Mackenzie was holding two cookies, and offered one to Sam. He smiled and took it, saying, "Thank you, Sweetie." The little girl lit up in a smile, and Indie helped her climb up on the couch.

"The remote's over there on the coffee table," Sam said around a mouthful of chocolate chip cookie. "Put something on she'll like, and we can talk about the case."

Indie turned on the big TV that hung on the wall, and shortly after, there were cartoons on the screen. The little girl was delighted, and began laughing and pointing at the screen.

"She hasn't seen a lot of TV lately," Indie said. "Even when we had our apartment, we didn't have one. The only time she got to watch cartoons was when I could get on the neighbor's wifi and get online. Cartoon Network dot com. The shows are stupid, but at least they're entertaining and keep her calm."

Sam nodded. "I guess," he said. "Never had much experience with 'em. You ready to go over this mess?"

She settled into the corner of the couch closest to him, and dragged her laptop out of its case. "Yeah, what have we got? Wait, you got wifi here?"

Sam nodded. "I do, but you need the password. Tell me when you're ready and I'll give it to you."

Indie tapped a few keys, and then looked up. "Okay, ready."

"The password is, and this is all one long word with no punctuation, youdontneedmystinkingpassword."

Indie looked at him and grinned as she typed it in. When it logged her onto his network, she shook her head. "That is probably the best password I've ever seen."

"It works," Sam said. "Okay, then, we've got a missing twelve-year-old girl named Cassie Rice. Her father, who has visitation with her every other Saturday, is Allen Rice, a known drug dealer who works with a web-based outfit known as drugspot dot org. What we think is that it has a back end that allows drug dealers to connect with their buyers secretly, so that they make their purchase through some online payment service, then the dealer just drops off their order."

Indie nodded. "Yeah, I've heard about things like this. They use a lot of different bots to move the money around, flipping it through Paypal, Goldmoney, Payeer,

Bitcoin, all of them. Makes it impossible to trace, they think. Not just drug dealers, lots of people who want to hide money, or hide where it comes from." She was tapping keys as she spoke. "Let's start with the daddy. What's his name again? Allen Rice, right? Any idea where he lives?"

Sam thought for a moment. "Yeah, Princeton Drive. That's not as nice a neighborhood as it sounds like."

"I know, I lived on College, just a block away. Pretty rough area, not good for kids." She looked at her daughter. "She likes to go outside and play, and I notice you've got a nice yard. Will it be okay if I let her out during the daytime?"

"Sure," Sam said. "Just keep an eye on her, there's a pool out there. I'll let the neighbors know I've got company, and they'll all watch out for her, too. This is a good neighborhood, by the way. There are some other kids around, too. I know there are some around her age a couple doors down." He pointed in the direction of the house he was referring to. "The Mitchells have two kids, twins, and they're about the size of yours, there."

Indie was looking at her screen. "Okay, I've got Allen Rice, found him on Facebook and got his email. Give me a little time, and I can tell you just about anything about him you might want to know." She continued tapping away. "So, you said you were married, once. Didn't work out?"

Sam grimaced. "Not exactly, but it was sort of a

mutual thing. I was more married to my job than I was to her, and she didn't like being at home alone all the time. One day I came home and found out I had the place all to myself. That was about nine years back."

"Sorry," Indie said. "Must suck, if you weren't expecting it."

Sam grinned. "Pretty much. On the other hand, almost every other cop I know has been through that or worse, with divorce, custody fights over kids and that kind of stuff. I think maybe I got off easy, cause there weren't any kids and she didn't even ask for anything. I let her take the car I'd bought her, and I paid for it, but other than that, it was all pretty simple."

Indie was looking closely at something on her screen. "How long has it been since anyone saw this Allen character?" she asked.

"Not sure; probably not more than a day or so, I'd guess. Why?"

"Because a bunch of people on Facebook have been trying to get his attention since the day before yesterday, and he hasn't logged on. That's odd, since I can scroll back and see that he checks in several times a day, normally. Give me a minute..." She went back to tapping steadily.

Sam thought about it for a moment, then took out his phone and called Sandy Ward.

"Mrs. Ward, it's Sam Prichard. You said your granddaughter went with her father on Saturday?"

"Yes, that's right," the woman said. "She was supposed to be back here by seven that evening, and hasn't been home since."

"Okay, and when was the last time you talked to her father?"

"Well, that would have been the same night. I called him around eight or so, cause he's late sometimes, and he said he dropped her off in front of my house at seven. I've tried to call him a few times since then, but he never answers."

Sam thanked her and hung up, then repeated the information to Indie. "Sounds like this guy may have split, after all. Mrs. Ward had said she didn't think Cassie was dead because her dad hadn't run away, but if he can't be found..."

"Then it doesn't sound good, right?" Indie asked, and Sam made a sad face.

"Not good at all," he said. "You say he hasn't been online, either?"

"That's not what I said," Indie pointed out. "I said he hadn't been on Facebook, and there's a big difference. He has, however, checked his email every day, and even just a few hours ago."

"How can you tell that?"

"Cause I figured out his password and I'm in his email account right now. Since I can see that most of the emails have been read, and several of them are only a few hours old, it's a safe bet he was in here today."

Sam's eyebrows were high. "Any info in there?"

"Not a lot, but I do see that he's out of town somewhere. The IP address he's logging into his email from is different from the local one, so he's definitely gone someplace. On the other hand, this is the email associated with his Facebook, so I've put in a request to reset his password. Soon as I get that, I can go into his Facebook and see who he's been talking to there. That might lead us to where he's gone, if he's got friends out around the country who log on from that same IP."

The reset came a few moments later, and Indie logged in to Rice's Facebook account. She poked around for a few moments, then started going through his message inbox.

"Okay, this is interesting," Indie said. "Up until he disappeared, Rice had been messaging a lot of people, mostly locals and most of them over and over, about the same thing, namely 'drop offs.' Pretty sure that alludes to dropping off some recreational drugs, wouldn't you think?"

"Most likely. Any kind of ID on who the buyers are?"

"Oh, heck, yeah, I've got the whole list. These idiots put all their info out there for anyone to snatch. Where do we wanna start?"

Sam leaned over and looked at the screen, as she showed him the several hundred friends of Allen Rice. Most of them, it seemed, were also customers, and he sat there for a moment thinking about where to begin.

"Are all of them local? Are there any who might be from wherever he's at now?"

"I'm checking," Indie said. "Nope, all I've got are local folks. He's got a few people on his friends list from other places, but no recent chats with any of them, so I'd bet he's not visiting any of them, either."

"I've got an idea," he said, and got up out of his chair to hobble toward his dining room. His computer desk was in there, and he grabbed a stack of paper from the printer and began laying it out on the table. He noticed Indie had followed him and was watching. "What I'm gonna do is set up a flow chart. Let's go through all of his deals that we can and see who he goes to most often, that sort of thing. Why don't you bring your computer in here, and we can get started tonight."

Indie shrugged and went to get her laptop, checking on little Mackenzie as she did so. She came back quietly a moment later and took the chair beside him. "Kenzie's out like a light. She usually won't fall asleep until she's snuggled up next to me; she must feel safe here."

Sam grinned. "Good, because you can both feel safe here. Now, let's make a list of his customers and see if we can figure out which ones he talks to most frequently..."

Indie slid her laptop in front of him, and he saw a spreadsheet laid out on it, with names and email addresses, along with dates and times. "That would be all of these in the first twenty-odd rows. I copied his friends list and scanned through his chats to get the times and dates when they talked, then had the computer put it all together in this format. Does that help?"

Sam stared at the screen, then realized that each entry had a link attached. When Indie clicked one to show him what it did, a box opened up that held the actual chat conversation from that particular time.

"Okay, and why is it the police don't hire people like you?"

Indie grinned at him. "I'm guessing that would be because the police would have to get a warrant to do what I'm doing, and that isn't always so easy to do. Hey, I told you, I'm a gray hat. I'm honest as they come in my own way, but laws are meant to keep people honest, and when they don't, then they're just in the way! If you can't live with that, then I need to shut down and leave now."

Sam stood still for a moment and looked at the screen. "I can live with it. Heck, I can even be grateful for it. So, these are his most common customers? Can you get me real IDs on them all?"

"Already did." She clicked another link, and a different spreadsheet appeared. This one had names and addresses, and even some phone numbers. "Here they are."

Sam shook his head in amazement. "Wow," he said. "What I coulda done with you, back when I was on the force!"

She sneered. "Back then, you probably would have at least thought about arresting me. I like you better this way." She pointed at the screen. "So, what else do you need to know? I can sort the data just about any way you might wish."

Sam looked at the screen for another moment, then pointed at his desk. "My printer is wireless; can you print this stuff out, and then let's start printing out info on each of the top twenty, so we can build a pattern out of it all. If we can find the patterns, then we can find the source of the patterns."

Indie looked at the printer and turned it on, then went to her laptop and tapped on the keys. A moment later, the first of the spreadsheets began spitting out on a number of sheets. The others followed, and then Indie was printing out individual pages on each of the people Rice had been dealing to through his Facebook account: Jason Burgess, John Merrell, Steve Wilson, Connie Miller and sixteen more. Each of them had a photo of the individual, base information like name, email, and address (if Indie could find it), phone numbers, and any other info she could dig up that seemed relevant. Some of them included arrest records and aliases, courtesy of public records databases that Indie had hacked her way into.

"How do you get all this info so fast?" Sam asked her, as the sheets kept spitting out. Each one he looked at amazed him for all the data he saw on it, more than most cops ever have available to work with.

"I don't," she said. "I let Herman do it. Herman's a program I wrote; I gave him all the passwords for the databases I use, and then when I feed him a profile, he'll take the names and info off of it and check through all of them. When he finds something that's a ninety-five percent match or better, he puts it into his report. Those reports are a lot like what you're seeing now."

Sam looked at the report in his hand—Marvin Dennis —and then looked back to Indie. "Herman did all this work? In a matter of seconds?"

She nodded. "Yep. He's fast."

"Yeah! No wonder you found me so quickly. I should hire Herman and let you go!"

Her eyes darkened. "Don't even think about it, Herman is loyal! We're a team, me and him!"

"Okay, fine, then," Sam said with a laugh. "But you pay Herman out of your share! I don't need to keep adding people to my payroll!"

They kept going over Herman's reports, and it wasn't hard to determine which of the customers were Rice's regulars. They were using tape to stick significant reports to one wall of the dining room, and Sam had found some string to use to indicate connections between different individuals. The five most common contacts went into one group, and Sam planned to start visiting them the following morning.

By the time they got their game plan laid out, it was nearly one AM. Sam had noticed Indie yawning. "You're tired. Why don't you go on to bed, and we'll work on this tomorrow. I'm gonna get up early and start on these first creeps, so you can sleep in. We'll talk when I get back and you're awake."

She smiled. "Thanks. The shelters make you get up at five thirty and eat breakfast, and then you gotta stay out 'til after seven that night and hope you're in line to get a spot to sleep. We were up early the last few mornings, and I don't sleep well in crowds of people I don't know." She walked to the living room and picked up her daughter, then carried her carefully up the stairs.

Sam went around and turned off lights, then made his way to his own bedroom. As he did so, he heard the shower start upstairs, and it occurred to him that it was kind of nice, having other people around. He hoped he'd still feel that way in three days, which was about as long as he'd ever lasted before with visitors until they got on his nerves.

He tossed off his clothes and pulled on the shorts he always slept in, then let himself lay back and relax. He was asleep within seconds.

Upstairs, Indie was enjoying the first really hot shower she'd had in weeks, and wishing she'd bought some new shampoo; the bottle she had was getting pretty low, and the only thing she found in the bathroom was a bottle of "Men's 2 in 1" that was so old it was crystallized. She'd have to scrape through the change she had left and see if there was enough for something generic.

There were towels, though, big fluffy ones that looked brand new. The top one had been pretty dusty, but the rest were fine, and she enjoyed the feeling of the one she was using against her skin. She'd give Kenzie a bath tomorrow, she thought, and let the little girl feel how nice the big towels were, too.

She slid into shorts and a t-shirt, then went back to the bedroom where Kenzie was sleeping already, climbed into bed, and whispered a short prayer of thanks to God for this break.

Sam's room was in the back of the house, which meant that the window on that wall was facing due east. That was fine by Sam, who hated to sleep late in any case, and so the sun coming through the window was better than an alarm clock. His eyes fluttered open, and he realized that it was morning.

He threw off the covers and reached for his cell phone, plugged into the charger he kept on the nightstand. The time display on it told him that it was already past seven, so he'd managed to sleep through some of the sunrise. A quick trip to the bathroom got him feeling more alive, and then he decided to finish it off with a shower.

Sam was a guy who sang in the shower, and he completely ignored the fact that there were others in the house. Something had him feeling so good that he launched into his own version of "Don't Worry, Be Happy," which was nothing like the original in any way.

He sang through it twice during his shower, and was still humming it when he made it to the kitchen fifteen minutes later.

He froze as he entered, because there was something in the air that was unfamiliar to him. It was—it was—was that the combined smells of fresh coffee and bacon?

"Morning, Sunshine," Indie said from over by the range. "I couldn't sleep, and neither could Kenzie, so we decided to make breakfast."

"We're makin' breakfast!" said Kenzie, sitting on a stool beside her mother. Sam couldn't hold back a big grin at her delighted smile.

"You are?" he asked the little girl. "Well, now, I don't know what to say! Nobody's made me breakfast in a long time! Are you gonna eat breakfast with me?"

The little blonde smiled from ear to ear as she nodded her head vigorously. "Uh-huh, me and Mommy!"

Indic was smiling at their exchange. "I warned you," she said. "She likes you already! Go ahead and sit, and I'll get you a cup of coffee."

Sam's hip gave him more trouble in the mornings than any other time, and was hurting, so he took her up on the offer. When he'd gotten himself into a chair at the kitchen table, Indie handed him a cup of coffee and a spoon. The sugar was on the table where he kept it, so he added his usual and stirred, then took a big sip.

"There's something about a cup of coffee that you

didn't make yourself that always tastes better, you know?" he said, and Indie laughed.

"Yeah, well, this is the first coffee I've had in a while that wasn't either stale or too strong to drink. The stuff they give you in the shelters is some kind of acid; there's a theory that it's designed to dissolve the homeless, so that society won't have to deal with them anymore."

A few moments later, she slid eggs and bacon onto plates, and then took a tray of hot buttered toast out of the oven, where it had been staying warm. She put two slices on each plate, then set one in front of Sam while Kenzie pulled out a chair for herself next to him. Sam reached over to help her get it where she wanted it, while Indie set their own plates on the table and joined them.

"We say grace," Indie said. "Is that gonna bother you?"

"Not a bit," Sam replied, then folded his hands and closed his eyes as Indie and Kenzie did so.

"God is great," said Kenzie, "God is good, and we thank Him for our food, Amen!"

"Amen!" Sam echoed, and Indie smiled at him.

"Thanks. I'm trying to teach her to be thankful for what we do have, instead of upset over what we don't." She suddenly found her plate to be interesting, and stared at it. "Um, I was thinking, since you're gonna be out today for a while, would you mind if I did some of our laundry in your washer and dryer? And could I use some cleaning supplies to clean up the upstairs? It's kinda messy and dirty up there."

Sam frowned. "Well, of course, you can use anything I got, but I don't know what cleaning supplies there are. I have a lady who comes in once a week to clean down here, and she brings a bucket full of stuff with her. I can give you some money, and you can go get whatever you need. I'm sure we could stand to have that kind of stuff around, anyway, right?" He shoved another forkful of eggs into his mouth. "Now that I think about it, is there even any soap or shampoo up there? And do you need anything for Kenzie, like special soaps for little kids?"

Indie grinned and looked up at him again. "You haven't been around kids much, have you?"

"Only when I get invited to the Mitchells' place, lately, and that isn't often." He looked at Kenzie and reached over to tickle her under the chin, which made her laugh. "But I could get used to this one, I sure could!"

Kenzie smiled and looked at her mother. "Mommy, does that mean we can live here?"

Indie choked, but Sam laughed. "It means you sure can for now, anyway, Sweetheart. No more shelters, okay? You and your mom can stay here for as long as you need to, and Mommy can help me out with some things."

"See, Baby?" Indie said. "We prayed for God to give us someplace safe to stay, and He brought us to Sam! We can stay here for a while, and I can help Sam with something in return for him letting us stay."

The little girl nodded her head wisely. "God's like that," she said, and Sam and Indie both burst into laughter.

They enjoyed their breakfast together, and then Sam gave Indie another fifty dollars to use to buy cleaning supplies and other necessities. She and Kenzie went back upstairs to finish dressing for the day, and Sam headed out to the van. He fired it up and drove to Rice's address.

The old-town neighborhood was pretty run down and rough, but Sam had been there many times and wasn't too intimidated. He found the house and parked in front of it, climbed out and walked up to the door. There was a doorbell, but he didn't hear a sound when he pushed the button, so he knocked loudly.

A woman came to the door wearing only a long t-shirt, rubbing sleep from her eyes. "Yeah?" she said.

"I'm looking for Allen Rice," Sam said. "I was told he lives here. Is he around?"

She looked up at him. "Nope, he hasn't been back since Sunday. You with the others lookin' for him? I already told those guys, I don't know where he'd go, and he didn't leave no money or dope here."

Sam nodded, as if he already knew that. "Yeah, well, he may have made a big mess, and we're just trying to clean up a lot of loose ends. You don't mind if I take a look around, do you?"

The woman stood there looking at him for a moment, then stepped back and motioned for him to enter. "Not a bit. Come on in."

Sam stepped inside carefully, leaning on his cane more as a caution against whatever might be slippery on the floor than because of his hip, and made his way through the small house. There was a living room, two bedrooms, a kitchen and a bathroom, and it took him only minutes to know that there was nowhere in any of them where a grown man might hide. The bedrooms only had mattresses on the floor, and the only furniture of any size was a sofa in the living room. Even the refrigerator in the kitchen was one of the small, college-dorm-sized ones, but he peeked inside just to be safe.

"Listen," he said to the woman, "one of the problems he left us with is about his little girl. She's gone missing, and if the cops get to lookin' too close, things could get ugly. You don't know where she might be, do you? Or what might have happened to her?"

The woman's eyes went to the floor, and she said, "I don't know where she is, but he said she was gonna make him a lot of money. All I know is she's supposed to be back in a week, if everything goes the way he wants it to, and he said we'd have enough money to get out of this rat hole and move out to Vegas." She looked up at Sam. "I don't know anything other than that, but I've met the kid and she's okay. I hope he ain't done nothin' that's gonna get her hurt."

Sam nodded. "Yeah," he said, "me, too." He took a pen out of his pocket and found a slip of paper to write his cell number on. "If you hear from him and call me, there's a twenty in it for you. And just so you know, all I really care about is finding the kid."

She looked at his name there on the paper. "Sam Prichard," she said. "You used to be a cop, you're the one who got hurt last year, right? My dad's a cop, he talked about you. You know him, Bob Bennet?"

Sam smiled. "I know Bob, he's a good man. You're his daughter?" He wanted to ask her what had brought her down so far, but some things just were none of his business.

She glanced around and then nodded. "Yeah, I'm Carly—but it isn't something I talk about a lot, not around here, y'know? He's always tryin' to get me out of here, back on the straight and narrow. Maybe someday I'll make it. I'll call you if I hear anything." She shut the door, and the conversation was over.

He went back to the van and thought about his next move. He had a printout of Indie's work from the night before, showing him the names and addresses of the top five of Rice's customers. These were the ones who seemed to be trying hardest to reach him, so they were the ones Sam thought most likely to have some idea of what was going on. He scanned through them, deciding who was closest.

He parked the van outside the home of his first

contact, Jason Burgess. Jason had apparently made a number of buys from Rice over the past few months, and was looking to score again. Sam climbed out and went to the door, knocking "shave and a haircut" to see what reaction it would get.

The man who answered the door looked pretty rough, as though he hadn't been sleeping well lately. "Yeah?" was all he said.

Sam smiled. "You Jason?" The guy nodded. "I'm Sam Prichard, and I'm looking for a friend of yours, Allen Rice. Any idea how I might find him? It's kind of important."

The guy suddenly looked more alert and wary. "I don't know any Allen Rice. Who told you I knew this guy?"

Sam tried to look surprised. "Well, Allen told me," he said. "Allen said if anything ever happened to him, that you'd be the guy to go to. He's disappeared, and so here I am."

The guy shook his head as if trying to clear it. "Wait a minute," he said. "Allen told you to come to *me*, if something happened to him? Why would he do that? I don't know nothin' about his business, and he didn't leave anything here with me."

Sam smiled. "Okay, good, so you do know him, and you know he's disappeared with money and dope that isn't his. Now we're getting somewhere. Tell me what else you know, Jason, like what you know about his little girl who's missing."

Jason's eyes got wide, and he started looking around as if trying to find something to say to get him out of whatever mess he was getting into. "No, look, man, all I know is there's other people askin' about where'd he go, and where's the stuff, and I don't know none o' that! He was supposed to bring me some stuff day before yesterday, and never showed, so that's all I know."

Sam leaned forward until his nose was only an inch from Jason's. "Okay, that's cool," he said, "but just for fun, lemme tell you this: if it turns out you know anything about the little girl, and you don't tell me, then I'm gonna come back, and you will not enjoy my next visit. So get on your computer and spread the word, there's a guy comin' around looking for that child, and if I don't find her soon, it's a pretty safe bet that the whole list I've got of all of Allen's customers is gonna end up in the hands of the DEA. Got all that?"

Jason's eyes were wide, and he nodded his head rapidly. "I got it, man, but I swear, I don't know nothin' about the kid! If I did, I'd tell you right now!"

Sam pulled out his pen and reached over to grab Jason's hand, then wrote his name and number across the palm. "If you hear anything about the kid, or about where Allen is hiding, I want to hear it a minute later. If I find out you didn't call me, or if I find out you waited two minutes to call me, I will be back to see you, and you will not like it." He let go of Jason's hand and smiled, then turned and walked back to his van.

4

The rest of Sam's morning was similar, but around ten thirty, he noticed that people seemed not to be so surprised when he showed up at their doors or workplaces. They also seemed less inclined to talk to him, so he was beginning to think he was shaking someone up. If he could find out who that was, he might get a little closer to learning what had actually happened to Cassie.

By noon, he was out of what he considered serious leads, and decided to go home. He called Indie's phone, and she answered on the first ring.

"Road Kill Cafe, you kill 'em, we grill 'em!"

Sam laughed. "Oh, Lord, I haven't heard that since I was a teenager! Listen, it's Sam; I'm heading back to the house and was thinking about grabbing something for lunch. You guys like pizza?"

Indie chuckled. "Have you ever known a girl who didn't like pizza? Of course we do! Supreme, if you can handle it!"

"I can, that's my fave. I'll swing around and bring

home a giant one. What about drinks? I'm into root beer, myself."

"That'll work for us, too. And don't be shocked when you get home, I've been cleaning, and you need to fire your cleaning lady! The gunk I got out of your carpet and kitchen counters? Grrr-*oss!*"

Sam grinned. "We'll talk about it when I get there. Bye!"

He called his favorite pizza parlor, a small independent shop that beat all the chains he'd ever tried, and ordered their giant supreme with a couple of big jugs of root beer. They told him it would be ready in twenty minutes, so he drove slowly in that direction.

He called Dan while he was poking along.

"Hey, Buddy!" he said. "I've been shaking a few trees today, and you might hear some rumbles about it, as well. That guy Allen Rice I asked about? He seems to have vanished, and apparently a significant amount of merchandise and/or cash has gone into the wind with him."

"I'm already hearing it. Word is that you're making people nervous, claiming to have lots of info I'd like to get my hands on. Any truth to that rumor?"

"Am I making people nervous? Yes. Do I have any such info? I do. Are you gonna get it? Yes, as long as you don't ask too many questions about how I came by it."

"Came by what? I don't know what we're talking

about. So how is this fitting into your hunt for a missing kid?"

"Allen Rice is a small-time dealer for this online outfit, I think, but he seems to be trying to get bigger. He told his girlfriend that his daughter would be gone a few days, but that she was going to make him a lot of money, then he drops off the face of the earth with money and dope that belongs to the big guys. Sounds to me like he's going after a big score, something that'll move him up in the organization, and using the kid as some kind of collateral."

Dan let out a low whistle. "I've heard of things like that," he said, "but I didn't think I'd ever come this close to a scumbag who'd do it. Any leads on where she is, yet?"

Sam shook his head automatically, even though he knew his friend couldn't see the gesture. "Nothing. I'm hoping that someone will decide to talk to try to keep me quiet about Allen's little black book, which they all think I've got. It's not that good, but it's worth some brownie points."

"You get it to me, and I'll see you get the points. Just let me know if you need anything, okay?"

"You got it," Sam said, and hung up. He pulled into the pizza shop a few minutes later and got his purchase through the drive-up window, then headed for home.

It suddenly hit him that this would be the first time in more than nine years that he would be going home and finding someone there, other than his mother or his sister on one of her rare visits. Sam had resigned himself to being alone while he was a cop, because so many cops had a hard time making relationships work. Wives hated the waiting, and dreaded the midnight phone calls, so they didn't usually manage to stick it out for long.In spite of his scattered attempts at dating after the shooting, he still couldn't quite see himself with a wife and family. Maybe someday, he thought, but not anytime soon.

He pulled into his driveway and parked next to Indie's Taurus. As he climbed out of the van, carefully balancing the pizza on one hand and holding the bag with the root beer in the other, Mrs. Tanner said hello to him over the hedge that separated his place from hers.

"Hello, Sam!" she called. Mrs. Tanner was about seventy and pretty lonely, so whenever she saw him outside, she was sure to call out and chat for a moment, and he never let it bother him.

"Hey, Mrs. T! How you been?"

"Oh, I'm fine," she said, "but I see you've got some company staying with you. Is that your girlfriend? She's awfully pretty!"

Sam laughed. "No, she's just a friend of mine who needed a place to stay for a bit. Yeah, she's a pretty little thing, that's true, but don't go tryin' to get rid of me, now, you know you're my sweetheart!"

The old woman smiled, but gave him a look that said he was full of it. "Sam, if I was forty years younger, I'd be all over you, boy, but I've seen those cougars on TV, and I can't live that way! You're safe, don't worry, but if that one is as nice as she seems, you better grab on while you can! And that little one she's got, she's just precious!"

"I'll bear that in mind, Mrs. T, but I don't think there's much to worry about there! I gotta go in, I brought home lunch! Wanna come join us for pizza?"

"Ha! No, thank you, you go on! That'd give me heartburn for days to come!"

Sam was still smiling as he went inside. Indie asked what had him so delighted, and he couldn't resist.

"Next-door neighbor, Mrs. Tanner. She must have spotted you on your way out this morning, because she's decided I need to marry you and make an honest woman of you."

Indie's eyes were wide, but she was smiling. "And did you happen to suggest to her that I might have something to say about that?"

Sam set the pizza down on the kitchen table. "I did better than that," he said. "I told her I couldn't marry you because I'm so in love with her, but she wasn't havin' me, either. Guess I'll just have to wait for Kenzie to grow up, and marry her."

Kenzie had come into the room when she heard his voice, and Sam reached down to tousle her hair, which got him a giggle. He picked her up and set her in a chair while Indie got out plates and glasses, then opened the box and put a slice on Kenzie's plate first.

They sat down together and Kenzie led them in saying grace, before Sam dug in. He had always liked pizza, and he got a kick out of watching the little girl eating hers.

"Well, we've got some people nervous," he said. "I'm not a hundred percent sure what's going on, but the way I'm reading things, Rice has used his daughter as some sort of collateral on a big drug deal; it looks like he's letting someone hold her in order to ensure he delivers on whatever it is he's doing, and that seems to be something that will make him a lot of money and get him a better spot in their organization. If we could figure out what that spot might be, we could be onto something big."

Indie shook her head. "If anyone told me I had to leave my daughter as a deposit for something, I think I'd kill 'em! That's disgusting!"

"It is, and it's even worse when you think about the kinds of things that might happen to a child in such a situation. I've known of people literally allowing others to abuse their kids in exchange for drugs and other things they wanted. I'm concerned about what little Cassie might be going through, and that makes me all the more determined to bring her home as soon as possible."

"Well, I had an idea," Indie said, "and maybe it'll help. I've got Herman scanning all over drugspot. Out on the surface, it's about getting information about prescription drugs, you know, but there are several hidden links that lead to different sections. Herman can spot those, and follow them, and that way we can find which ones lead into the back end, where we can find out more information. Then I'll try to figure out Allen's login and password, and we'll go from there. If I can get into his account there, we should be able to find out a lot more about what he's doing, and what drugspot does."

Sam smiled. "You're quite a whiz with that computer stuff, aren't you?"

"Yep. Now if only I could find a job doing it, I'd have it made!"

"Well, you've got one for right now. Let's eat up, then see what old Herman's been doing, okay?"

"Huh-uh, not 'til you let me show you how bad your housekeeper's been ripping you off! I don't know what you're paying her, but it's way too much; as far as I can tell, all she's doing is sweeping dirt under the carpet and slinging a dirty mop and rag around in your kitchen, and I am *not* kidding!"

"Hmm. She came highly recommended, too, by my mother. Mom's a real estate agent, and this gal cleans up empty houses for her. She doesn't cost a whole lot, but if you want the job, I'd be willing to talk about it."

Indie froze and looked at him for a moment. "You mentioned something yesterday, about housekeeping in exchange for room and board. Is that offer on the table? I keep the place clean, and me and Kenzie get to stay here?"

Sam thought it over. "I could go along with that, but there isn't that much cleaning to do. I guess that would leave you free to get another job, if you wanted to..."

Indie nodded. "That's what I was thinking," she said. "If I knew we had a place to stay, then I could get a real job and put some money away so we could get our own place, sometime."

Sam nodded and extended a hand. "Deal. But don't go job hunting 'til we get done with this case, okay? I'll pay for your time on it, no problem, and if you need some cash in the meantime, just say so."

They shook hands, and Sam made a note to call his mother and tell her she didn't need to come help with cleaning his house any longer. He just hadn't wanted to admit to Indie that the cleaning lady was his mom, and that it was actually him who'd been sweeping stuff under the carpet.

When their lunch was over, they went to the dining room, while Kenzie got to go out into the backyard and play for a while. There was a privacy fence that went all the way around, and the pool was secured with a safety fence around it, so there was nothing out there that would be likely to cause an injury. They left the big sliding glass doors open and listened as she played.

Indie pulled up Herman, and let Sam see what it was doing. "Another part of Herman is a search program that allows me to put in various criteria that I want him to look for. That way, I can tell him to look for things, like people who are all friends with Allen Rice on Facebook and also have Sam Prichard as a friend. Surprisingly, you guys have three mutual friends, though I suspect they're just people who friend everyone; there's a lot of those out there. Anyway, he can also scan every bit of text or code or imagery on a website and look for hidden links, back doors, gateways and such, and when he finds them, he tries to figure out how to get past them. That's what I've had him doing since I got back from the store this morning, so let's get his report." She tapped the keyboard rapidly, and then sat back to watch as line after line of text began to appear on the screen. She was reading it as fast as she could, silently, and running a finger along each line as it appeared.

"Okay, we've got some pay dirt, here. Herman found an unsecured back door into a directory called 'freightliners,' and from what I'm seeing, it's probably a listing of names and usernames for their dealers or delivery people. This link was a single period in the fine print in the footer of one page, so the chances of anyone other than a robot ever finding it without being told are slim to none! Let's see if we can find Mr. Rice—and there he is, big as life! His username is tinman!"

Sam stared at all of the data on the screen, and shook his head. "Indie, you're amazing. Now, does this mean we can get into his account?"

She shook her head in the negative. "Not just yet. Now we need his password, and that won't be in a list on the site. However, if he used his main email address..."

She began tapping keys again, and a moment later, a dark blue page appeared with only two white boxes. "This is the login page. We put in his username, tinman, and then we use his password from his email account— nope, that wasn't it, but we got lucky, and it has a lost password bot! So I put in his email address, and *yes!* It's sending him his password even as we speak!"

She opened another browser and brought up Rice's email account, then clicked on the email from drugspot.org. There was a link inside it, and she clicked that, as well, and then got another email that contained his password. She quickly deleted those emails.

"I'm getting rid of those, so he can't log in and see them. This way he doesn't know we got his passwords and can watch everything he's doing."

"Smart girl, aren't you?" Sam said, and she grinned up at him.

"One of the smartest!"

"I believe it. Let's see what we've got there!"

She went back to the original browser and entered the password into the box. The page began to refresh, and then there were more entry fields, with titles like District, Crew, Services and more. Some of them were simple text boxes, and others were checkboxes that allowed multiple selections; for instance, the section titled Services had possible selections like: NRCS, SXL, BMKT and other alphabet soups, and it was possible to select more than one at a time. Since they didn't know what Rice might be involved in, they were cautious.

Sam pointed to NRCS. "Narcotics, I'd bet," he said. "We know Rice is into drugs, so let's try that one."

"Okay, but what about crew and district and line? We don't know what they mean, let alone how he would enter the data."

"True, but we gotta try something. District is a drop-down list, so just check the first one, then same for crew and line. Can't be worse than it already is, right?"

Indie shrugged. "Okay," she said. She clicked on District, and selected "1," then on Crew and selected "A." Line didn't have any entries, so she ignored that, and continued choosing the first item she could in each of the other fields. When all of them had an entry, she hit the Submit Button at the bottom of the page.

Suddenly, they were looking at a page that appeared to be a collection of business programs. There were folders arranged all over the page, and each one had a title. The first was called "Accounting," and that was followed by "Marketing," "Receivables," "Payables" and then "Deliveries."

The one that caught Sam's attention, however, was titled "Communications, Internal," and he pointed to it. Indie clicked on it, and what looked like an email program popped open.

There were dozens of messages, each one either to or from Rice. They began looking at the ones that had already been read, and the story that unfolded before them was mind-boggling.

Allen Rice had dreams of being bigger in the organization, all right, and he didn't care what he had to do to get there. Some of the earliest emails between him and his supervisor were discussions about his insistence that he was smart enough to run a crew all by himself. The supervisor found this funny, apparently, and let Rice know that he didn't have anywhere near the brains it took to run a crew for the Company. Rice protested, over and over, that all they needed to do was give him a chance and he'd prove himself.

This had all begun weeks before, and every email seemed to be a mere continuation of the same theme. Rice demanded his chance; the supervisor denied it. Sam shook his head.

"Personally, I'd have shot the guy after the first week," he said. "I don't know how this supervisor had the patience to keep putting up with him all this time! I couldn't have done it!"

They continued reading, and suddenly struck gold. Only two weeks before, the supervisor finally made a proposal that Rice found interesting.

"I was out your way last weekend," the email read, "and saw you with a young girl. That would be your daughter, of course, whom you get to see every other Saturday. She's a pretty little thing, and I thought that perhaps you might be worth a try after all. If you were to arrange for her to come and stay with us for a few days, with no harm to come to her at all, of course, then I would see fit to let you have a shot at running a crew. We'd send you off to St. Louis to handle a specific situation for us. When you get back, if you've sold all your product and done well, then we'll give you a crew of your own to run out in Vegas. Your daughter would only be our guest until you got back from St. Louis, of course, and she'd be returned to you as soon as you come back with our money." The next few emails discussed the idea further, and the last one—dated the previous Friday—was Rice's agreement and promise to deliver his daughter the next day.

Sam shook his head. "That's what I figured," he said. "He used his daughter as security, so he could make some fast money."

"Man, that is sick," Indie said. "Can we hang this guy? I want to see him do time over this, especially if the little girl gets hurt!"

"Oh, I promise you," Sam said coldly, "this guy's going down, one way or another."

"Okay, look here," Indie said, pointing. "He says he'll drop her off at 'the old warehouse,' wherever that is. Let me see if there's anything here that gives us locations, but I'm sure they're smarter than that." She tapped at the keys for several minutes, pausing now and then to look at the screen, but finally, she shook her head. "No luck, I'm afraid."

Sam sat there and thought for a few moments. "What

about other users of this system? Can we identify anyone else? If we can get a lead on one of the others, maybe I can shake the location of that warehouse out of that one."

Indie nodded. "Give me a little time, I'll get someone!" Her fingers flew over the keys and the screen flashed back to the page full of names and usernames. "I've got Herman scanning for any name on here that matches one of Rice's Facebook friends. It's beyond any logic that of all the people he knows, he's the only one on here. I'd bet he's friends with at least one or two others who deal for this outfit."

A moment later, the computer made what Sam considered a triumphant *beep,* and two names appeared on the screen: Levi Stein and Matthew Bryant.

"Bingo!" Indie said. "Both of these guys are dealing, just like Rice. Odds on they'll know something about the warehouse, wouldn't you think?" She looked up at him excitedly, and for a brief second, Sam thought she was absolutely beautiful.

He shook it off. "Darn right," he said. "Get me their addresses and where they work, and I'll go see 'em!"

The girl nodded. "Give me five," she said, and went back to typing. A few moments later, the printer hummed to life, and she snatched a page from it. "Here you go. Both their addresses, and their jobs. Levi works at the Wal-Mart on Evans Avenue, and Matthew works for his dad's trucking company out on the edge of town,

Bryant Trucking."

Sam smiled a grim smile. "I think I'll go pay them a visit," he said. "Let's see what they know."

"Hey, hold up a minute," Indie said. "I just wanna check one more thing." Her fingers flew, and a moment later there was another report coming out of the printer. She looked at it and whistled. "Look at this," she said to Sam. "Levi and Matthew have both been arrested before, for the same attempted murder charge, but the witness disappeared and the charges got dismissed for lack of evidence. Other than that, they've both got rap sheets as long as your arm, and mostly for violent offenses."

She was right. Both of the men had been arrested numerous times for assaults, robberies, threatening and other forms of violence, and almost all of the charges were dismissed when victims changed their minds or witnesses failed to remember what they'd seen, or even to show up at all to testify. These guys were dangerous, and Sam was just a semi-crippled ex-cop.

He went to his bedroom and opened his bottom dresser drawer, then took out the lock-box he kept there. The key on his key ring opened it, and he withdrew the forty-caliber Glock he'd carried as a detective. He worked the action to make sure it was still well-lubed and free, then picked up one of the four loaded clips that were in the box beside it and slammed it home. He dug in the drawer again and found the clip-on holster and slipped it onto his belt, and the gun went back into its familiar place like it had missed being there.

He went back to the dining room and sat down beside Indie, then took out his phone and dialed a number. When he got an answer, he smiled.

"Is that Kimberly? Hey, Kiddo, it's Sam Prichard, how you been? I'm good—listen, I need a favor, and I know you're the gal who can do it. I'm going into the PI biz, and I need a Concealed Carry Permit. How long would it take me to get one? Girl, you are an absolute gem! I'll be there in a half hour!" He hung up and smiled at Indie. "That's the girl at the sheriff's office who tests people for their concealed carry permits, and she said if I can get there in a hurry, she'll get me in this afternoon's test and I can have my permit today. I gotta run."

He stood up, and that's when he noticed that Indie was staring at the gun on his hip. He looked down at it, then at her. "Is that gonna be a problem?" he asked. "I think I need to have it, if I'm gonna be doing this sort of thing, don't you? Especially with the kind of people we're looking at here?"

Indie sat there without speaking for moment, then shook her head. "It's no problem," she said. "The thought that you might need it just makes me a little bit nervous, that's all. I'll be okay."

He went out to the van and got in, then took off for the sheriff's office. The CCL tests were held at the sheriff's firing range, and he'd have to demonstrate his ability with the gun, but he wasn't worried. He'd passed every test with a handgun since he was eighteen years old, and knew without any doubt that he would be as good with it that day as he'd ever been.

He was right; an hour later, he had passed the test with flying colors, and his brand new CCL was in his wallet, with a sheriff's endorsement. With that, he could carry his weapon anywhere, since it made him a *de facto* deputy sheriff. Sam was once again a law enforcement officer.

He went into the courthouse and filed for a Private Investigator's License, as well. Colorado didn't actually require one, but they instituted a voluntary license in 2012. Having it didn't give any more authority, but it did lend a lot of credibility. Sam thought, since he was going to be carrying concealed, he might as well go all out and get the license that would justify it if he ever had to use his weapon in the course of an investigation. Because of his history as a police officer, he was granted his license and shield immediately, though he had to pay almost a hundred dollars for the latter.

He walked out into the sunshine and called Dan Jacobs. "Hey, Buddy, guess who just got tagged as a straight-up PI?"

"You? Sam, I think that's great. Keep you busy, and let you do some good. And you always got me to do the grunt work, right?"

Sam laughed. "Yep. Thanks, man, I just wanted to

tell somebody. I'll be in touch."

"You better be," Dan said. "You did promise me a copy of that info you got, remember?"

"I ain't forgot, don't worry. You'll have it within a few days or so."

He cut off the call, and then did the thing he'd been avoiding all day; he called his mother.

"Sam, my *God*! It's about time I hear from you, are you okay?"

"I'm fine, Mom, how you been?"

"Oh, my God, I'm just going *crazy* with the way real estate prices are dropping right now. It's terrible! So what blessed event has resulted in you giving your old mother a call?"

Sam grimaced. "Well, actually, Mom, there's a couple of things. First off, I got a new housekeeper, a girl who's gonna live in and take care of the place for me..."

"Sam! You got a girlfriend? Oh, that's wonderful! Tell me about her, is she a nice girl? She's not like your ex-wife, is she, I mean, that woman, oh! She was just so not right for you, Sam, and..."

"Mom? Mom! No, I don't have a girlfriend, Mom, she's just a girl I know who needed a place for her and her little girl to stay, and so we worked out a trade while she looks for a regular job and gets on her feet. That's all it is, but you don't need to come over to help me clean up anymore, it's covered now."

His mother seemed slightly offended. "Well, if that's what you want, then I guess that's fine, Sam, but do you really know this girl? She isn't some stray you picked up, is she, cause you know how you always used to bring home stray dogs and cats all the time, and it was always so heartbreaking for you when we had to get rid of them."

"She's not a stray, Mom, just a friend of mine who was down on her luck, and I've got all that room. Anyway, the other thing is that I've decided to go into the Private Eye business, and I just got my licenses today. I know you've got friends at the courthouse, so I wanted to tell you before any of them could."

"Well, Sam, I think that's wonderful! You need something to keep you busy, I've said that before! Maybe you can help some poor woman catch her husband cheating, God knows I wish I'd been able to catch your father, but then he didn't care, so..."

"Mom!" Sam yelled into the phone. "Mom? You're breaking up, I can't hear you! You gotta get a new phone, Mom, that one's..." He hung up.

She didn't bother to call back. She never did. He made his way back to the van, and then headed for Evans Avenue. Levi was probably at work right then, and what better place for the chat they were about to have than Wal-Mart?

5

Sam pulled up and parked in one of the handicapped spaces at Wal-Mart on Evans, and then climbed out and headed inside. He was using his cane, and it was helping, since his hip was acting up that day. He got inside and spotted a woman who was walking around with lots of keys and looked like she knew what she was doing, so he caught her attention.

"Excuse me, Ma'am," he said, flashing his new shield and ID. "My name is Sam Prichard, and I'm a private investigator. I'm looking for one of your employees, Levi Stein. Can you tell me where I might find him?"

The woman looked at his ID for a second, then took a walkie-talkie out of a pocket and called someone on it. "I've got a Detective here," she said, "looking for Levi. Is he back there?" She held the speaker to her ear and listened for a moment, then said, "Okay, thanks, I'll send him back." She put the talkie back in her pocket and said, "He's out back in receiving. If you go through the double doors at the back of this aisle, you'll see the loading docks. That's where you'll find him." She turned away as if Sam didn't even exist.

He walked down the aisle and out the double doors she'd indicated, then saw the loading docks at the end of a long hallway. There were forklifts and pallet jacks moving around with people operating them, and he had to dodge them to get by, but finally he saw Levi standing at the back of a semi-trailer. He walked up and flashed his ID.

"Levi, I'm Sam Prichard, private investigator. I'd like to ask you a few questions about Allen Rice."

Levi shrugged his shoulders. "Go ahead and ask," he said. "What can I tell you?"

"I'm trying to find Allen's little girl," Sam said bluntly. "I know that he gave her to someone in the drugspot organization, as security for some big deal he's doing. All I care about is getting the little girl back safely; nothing else matters to me right now. If you can help me do that, I can forget your name and everything else I know about you."

Levi was standing there calmly, and didn't seem the least bit concerned with what Sam might know. He grinned at him and said, "I don't know anything about that. I heard some rumor that Allen's getting a promotion, but I don't think it's for real, and if it is, he'll find a way to mess it up like he does everything else. Any idea who he gave the kid to?"

Sam was surprised at how open Levi was acting, and it made him wary. He looked around, but there was no one close enough to overhear them. "No. All I know is he was supposed to drop her off at something called the old warehouse. Any idea where that is?"

Levi sucked on his bottom lip for a moment, looking at the floor, then raised his eyes back to Sam's. "Only place might be called that is the building where the night shipments come in. If I give it to you, you'll forget me? Completely?"

Sam smiled, then crossed his heart with his finger. "Completely," he said. "And if it gets the kid back safe, I'll owe you one personally. Maybe you'll need a favor one day, maybe not, but it would be there."

Levi grinned. "I'm sure I'd need it sooner or later, but I can't be sure this is gonna get you what you need; no promises, but the place I think they call the old warehouse is down on Green Valley, near where it hits E 470. It's a big yellow building, adobe-looking thing. There's an office there, but the old guy who works there wouldn't know anything about the Company, so don't shake him up too bad. That's about all I can tell you, man, but I hope it works out for you."

Sam stared at him. "Thanks. Can you tell me why you're being so helpful?"

Levi looked back at him and grinned. "Sure," he said. "I want to see you find the kid, and get her out of the mess her daddy put her in, that's part of it; but the main reason is because I know who you are, Detective Prichard, and I'm the informant who gave your guys the info the day you got shot. I figure I owe you one, y'know? Now, I gotta get back to work."

Sam stood there for a moment as Levi walked away, then turned and made his way back through the store. Part of him wanted to get angry at that guy, make him pay for what happened that day, but he was just the source of the information. He didn't get the warrant, he didn't orchestrate the raid, he didn't do anything but let Carlson's people know that there was a major shipment due in, giving them a good chance to make a major dent in the local drug operations.

Sam let it go, and then got into the van and drove away. He started to call Dan as he did so, but changed his mind. He didn't have enough information to justify a warrant, and Carlson probably wouldn't let him be in on it anyway, so he decided to go check out the warehouse for himself.

Dan would probably shoot him if he knew about it.

An hour later, he drove the van up to the only building that fit Levi's description. There was indeed an office, and he walked up and knocked on the door there. An elderly man came and opened it.

"Can I help you, young feller?" he asked.

"Yes, sir," Sam said. "I think so. I heard a rumor this building might be coming up for lease sometime soon, and I was wondering if I could take a look around inside it?"

The old man looked surprised. "Up for lease? Oh,

goodness, I hope not! I've worked here nearly forty-five years, I'd hate to lose my job now!" He looked Sam up and down. "Well, you just never know, though, do you? Come on in, it can't hurt nothin' to let you look around, I guess."

Sam followed the man inside and let him lead the way into the big, empty expanse that was the old warehouse. There were several smaller rooms off to the sides, but all of them were empty and open.

"What's this place used for now?" Sam asked.

"Oh, they bring in some trucks now and then and unload stuff here, stuff that's going on to other places, I reckon. They sort it out and load it back on other trucks, and out it goes again, *zoom*! Like sortin' the mail, I guess, just decide where it goes and send it on its way."

Levi had been right; this old fellow didn't know much of anything, and he appeared to be a bit simple, anyhow. If this was the place where Rice had dropped his daughter off, there would be no sign of her presence left by then. Still, Sam couldn't just walk away.

"Say," he said, "I was wondering, do you know who the actual owner of the building is? I'd like to give a call and see if I can get a deal worked out before it gets away from me, y'know? And don't worry, if I can lease it, I'd still need someone to watch over it, so you'd still have a job if you want it."

The old guy looked a little confused for a moment, but then he brightened. "Oh, you must mean Mr.

Ingersoll! He's the owner, or at least, he's the one I talk to. I think there's several owners, you know, but Gene Ingersoll, he's the one who runs everything. Here, let me get you his phone number, it'll just take me a minute!" He went into his own little office and flipped through an old-fashioned Rolodex for a moment, then scribbled something onto a post-it note and brought it to Sam. "Here you go, that's his office number right there. And if you do lease it, then yeah, I'd sure like to keep my job if I can."

Sam smiled and took the note. "Thank you, sir, and I'll sure keep that in mind. You have a good day, now, okay?" He made it out of the building and into the van without any further delays, and then looked at the note in his hand.

Eugene Ingersoll, it read, with a phone number. Sam got out his phone and dialed it immediately.

"Hello?" said a voice that sounded highly cultured.

"Mr. Ingersoll?" Sam asked, and the man chuckled.

"Yes, this is Gene Ingersoll. May I ask who I have the pleasure of speaking to?"

Sam smiled. "Mr. Ingersoll, I'm Sam Prichard, a private investigator, and I'm trying to locate a missing child. I've been given to understand that you may have some knowledge of where that child is, and if you could tell me, I think it would be very good for both of us."

The laugh came again. "Well, first, Mr. Prichard, I'm certain that I don't have any such knowledge, so we're wasting a lot of time already. However, second, if I did, then I'm also certain that the mere stupidity of calling me this way and demanding it would be enough to ensure that I would keep it to myself, don't you think? Why on earth would I admit to knowledge that could put me in prison?"

"The short answer to that would be that I'm calling out of a desperate desire to see the child come home safely, and I was hoping you'd help. However, I'm also in possession of a great deal of information regarding a certain venture that you are almost certainly a part of, Mr. Ingersoll, and that information can be lost if I get that child back safely. If I don't, then that information, all of it, will make its way into the hands of some people who would probably like to ruin your day for the rest of your life. I hope that allows us to understand each other, sir, and that it will make it possible for us to work together to bring this situation to a mutually satisfactory conclusion."

The man on the other end burst out into raucous laughter, and the cultured accent became less noticeable. "Well, well, you went straight for the jugular, there, didn't you? Now, assuming that I do have any involvement in that venture you're speaking of, what kind of assurance do I have that you're a man of your word? And assuming I did know anything about that missing girl, of course."

Sam grinned. "The only assurance I will give you, sir, is this: you just slipped and told me that you do know exactly what I'm talking about, which makes you an accessory to kidnapping at the very least. If you give me the kid, and she is safe, then that will be the very last you ever hear of me. If you don't, then I can guarantee you that I'll have the DEA crawling up your ass within a matter of days, and whatever they don't tear to shreds, I will! I'm a private investigator, Ingersoll. I'm not a cop, not anymore. My job is to find and recover that girl, not to get into your business. If I achieve my goals with your help, then your business stays your business. If not, then I'll make it my business to destroy you. Do we understand each other?"

Ingersoll was quiet for a few seconds, then said, "Mr. Prichard, you play a dangerous game, but I can say this. I know about the girl you're looking for, but I don't have her, and I don't know where she is. To do what you want will take some time, a day, maybe. If you can give me that long, I'll try to help you out, and I'll trust—for now—that you'll honor your end of this bargain. I'm sure you know enough to know that if you don't, it will cost you your life, am I right?"

"I know that's how you see it, but I'm notoriously hard to kill. So you want me to call you in twenty-four hours?"

"No need to call me at all, Mr. Prichard, I have caller ID just like you do. I'll call you as soon as I know something. And I won't promise you that there won't be some additional price for our cooperation, so bear that in mind. Don't worry, it wouldn't be money; we just might need your services at some point in time. If that addendum were to be presented as part of getting you what you want, would you be agreeable?"

Sam thought it over. "My legitimate services, sure. Just don't ask me to break any laws for you."

Ingersoll laughed again. "I wouldn't dream of it, Mr. Prichard. Now, go home and wait for my call; it may come sooner than you think."

The line went dead, and Sam felt a shiver run down his spine. He was pretty sure he'd just spoken to one of the actual heads of the Hydra that ran the drug operation they'd been trying for years to shut down, and there was no doubt in his mind that the man he'd just talked to could order his death with a single phone call.

On the other hand, Ingersoll had made it clear that he was more interested in having Sam indebted to him than having him dead. That alone made Sam think he had a chance of getting the girl back safely, and living through it at the same time. Just the knowledge that the Hydra was willing to discuss returning the girl meant that she was probably alive and relatively intact. That meant there was a chance, and that was more than he'd have thought he could say that morning.

He started up the van and drove toward home. He'd made his contact, and now it was just a matter of waiting for the response. He drove into his driveway just before five thirty, and made his way inside.

The smell got him first; he hadn't smelled anything

that good in so many years that he'd forgotten what it was! It was coming from his kitchen, of course, and he followed his nose to see what it could be. Indie was standing there at the stove, her back to him as she stirred something in a large pot, and she jumped when he said, "I hope that's supper cooking, and there better be enough for me!"

"Oh! Geez, don't do that, you scared the life outta me! Yes, it's supper and there's plenty; I found a small roast in your freezer, and some canned veggies that looked like they had ten years' dust on 'em, and made a stew. I hope that's okay."

He grinned as he limped over and sniffed at the pot. "It's fine. I bought that roast a few months ago, when I thought I was gonna have a date over for dinner one night, but she backed out and I never got to use it. The cans aren't that old, but they probably were pretty dusty. Smells delicious! Where's Kenzie?"

"Oh, Mrs. Mitchell came down and introduced herself, said Mrs. Tanner told her about us, and she invited Kenzie to come and play with her twins for a while. They're all the same age, so it's great, and I got a break for the first time in, like, forever! She said she'll bring her back down around six thirty, so I'm timing dinner for about then. Hope you can hold out that long."

"I'll manage, but it won't be easy, as good as that smells. Meanwhile, let's talk while we wait. Got any coffee left? I could use a cup."

"No, but it only takes ten minutes." She started setting up a pot of coffee, and Sam sat down at the kitchen table. He glanced around the kitchen, and said, "You know, I think I've spent more time in there these past two days than in the past year."

Indie looked at him. "Okay, you know that's kinda sad, right?"

Sam looked at her and grinned. "I prefer to think of it as more poignant than sad. Sad makes it sound, I dunno—sad! Poignant sounds more like something big is coming down the pike, and it just hasn't got there yet!"

Indie shook her head at him. "No, it's just sad. The kitchen is supposed to be the place where a home lives, y'know, and to not even go into it on a daily basis, that's just..."

"Yeah, I know," Sam interrupted. "It's sad!"

Indie laughed. "So, tell me how things went for you today, while I wait for your coffee."

Sam sighed. "You're not gonna believe it, but I think I've got a good chance of getting Cassie back safe. I went and got my CCL and then I figured I might as well be legal, so I got my PI license, too, and then I went to see Levi Stein. Believe it or not he's a decent sort, in his own way, and opened right up and told me what I wanted to know about the warehouse. I went down and checked it out, and managed to get the old guy who works there and knows absolutely nothing to give me the owner's name and number. I called that guy, and he said there was a good chance he could get me the girl back, but it would take time, and may leave me owing him a favor. I told him if I got her back safe, fine; if not, I was gonna ruin his whole life!"

Indie was staring at him with her mouth hanging open. "Sam, holy crap! You coulda got yourself killed!"

"Yeah, he said something like that, too, and I reminded him that it isn't something that's all that easy to do. I'm a tougher old bird than you might think; I mean, I lived through the last time they tried to kill me, right?"

Indie scowled at him. "That's like saying, hey, I got away with murder once, I can get away with it again! That's stupid, Sam. I may not know you all that well, but I do kinda like you, and I don't wanna see you get hurt. Besides, what would that do to my living arrangements? I need you alive and well so I can live here, remember?"

The coffee was done a few moments later, and she poured him a cup and brought it to him. He fixed it up and took a sip, then said, "So, you can clean, and now I find out you can cook, too. How much would it cost me to just keep you here as my housekeeper and cook?"

Indie blinked. "Are you being serious?" she asked.

He shrugged. "That depends on the answer. If I can afford it, then yeah, I'm being serious."

Indie stared for a moment, then said, "Well, you're already providing me with room and board, so if we just take off what I'd have to pay for rent and utilities and groceries, then I could do it for about a hundred and fifty a week. Is that too much?"

Sam grinned. "For a buck and a half a week, I can get cooking like this every day? You got a deal, girl!" He shoved his hand out for her to shake, and she took it nervously.

"Sam, can you really afford that? Aren't you on like a pension or something?"

"My medical retirement is seventy-five percent of my pay at the time of the shooting, with bi-annual cost-of-living increases, so it's not that bad," he said, "but then there's the hazardous duty coverage; that pays me another twelve hundred a month, just because I got shot in the line of duty. I can pay you outta that and never touch my pension!"

Indie shook his hand again. "Then you've got yourself a cook and housekeeper! Sam, you really were a Godsend, you know that? I don't know what would have happened to me and Kenzie if you hadn't placed that ad when you did."

Suddenly, there were tears falling down Indie's cheeks, and Sam reached across the table without thinking to place his hand on hers.

"Indie," he said, "what is it that you haven't told me? Is there something that's gonna come back to bite you in the butt? Or me?"

She shook her head and even managed a laugh. "No, there's nothing like that. It's just that—Sam, when I got back here from MIT, I moved back in with my mom, and it didn't go well. She had a boyfriend, and he thought since I was my mother's daughter, I must be as easy as she was. When he tried to get friendly with me, I sorta beat him half silly with mom's portable mixer. He was screaming like a banshee, and she came running to see what was wrong with him, and when I told her what happened, she threw me and Kenzie out. I was working at Dairy Queen, then, and had a little money saved up, so I got an apartment for us, but then the manager wanted me to date him and when I said I didn't date my boss, he found a reason to fire me—said I showed up late three times in a row, by changing the schedule after the fact. I haven't been able to get another steady job, and that's how I lost the apartment, and ended up in the shelters. It's a miracle no one called CPS on me." She wiped her eyes. "So, yeah, if you hadn't come along when you did, I don't know where Kenzie and I would be now."

Sam sat there for a moment. "What happened to Kenzie's father? Is he around?"

She made a sound that was another half sob, half laugh. "No, that's another whole story. His name was Jared MacKenzie, which tells you who my daughter is named for. He was my high school sweetheart, and we were actually planning to be married once I got out of college. He wanted to join the Marines, so he figured he'd get his basic training and AIT all over with while I went to college, and then we'd get married as soon as possible after that. Of course, we were sleeping together, and I guess birth control isn't as foolproof as they want you to believe it is, because a couple months after he shipped out for boot camp and I went to MIT, I woke up to morning sickness! I hadn't even skipped a period, so it was a real surprise, y'know? I wrote to him and told him I was pregnant, and he called me the night he got the letter, all excited. He said he wanted to get married as soon as he got out of AIT, which would have been in five more months, but then he was killed in an accident during his training. He hadn't even gotten a chance to make any provision for me or the baby, so I was SOL and all on my own."

"Wow," Sam said. "You've had it tough, girl. What about his folks, don't they want to be part of his daughter's life?"

"Not exactly. They blame me for his decision to join the Marines, because I was going to college and he couldn't afford to; they think he only joined to show me he was a real man, y'know? And since that's how he died, they blame me for that, too."

Sam shook his head. "Maybe one day they'll come around," he said lamely.

There was a knock on the front door, and Anita Mitchell came in with Kenzie. "Hi, Sam," she said, then turned to Indie. "Indie, she was a little angel! She can come down anytime, just holler! Tracy and Lacey loved having her over, and she did me a favor cause they're worn out and down for a nap, now!"

Indie smiled. "I'm glad she behaved herself," she said. "And the same goes for you. Anytime you need a break, I'm willing to watch all three sometimes—if it's okay with you, Sam?"

Anita smiled. "Ignore Sam, he's a big pussycat! He won't mind; he's actually watched them for me a couple times, himself!"

Sam grinned. "Nope, I don't mind a bit. Tell Jim I said hi."

Anita smiled and waved as she left. "I will," she called over her shoulder as she went out the front door again.

Kenzie climbed up into the chair beside Sam and smiled up at him. "Did you know they got a doggie, a great big one, and it's got babies?"

"They do?" Sam asked. "And did you get to play with the puppies?"

"Yeah, and I got to go in their yard and see the babies, and they let me hold one of 'em, and it licked me right up my nose!"

Sam laughed, and Indie joined in. "Right up your nose? Oh, no!"

"Oh yeah, and it tickled!"

Sam and Kenzie continued to talk about puppies and tickles while Indie got plates and began putting dinner on the table. The stew smelled delicious still, but when she ladled it over buttered Texas toast, Sam thought he'd died and gone to Heaven! The beef, carrots, onions and potatoes all blended together to make an awesome meal, and he was delighted to see that there would be plenty of leftovers.

When dinner was over, they all went into the living room and turned on the TV. This time, Indie chose a movie that she'd wanted to see, and managed to get Kenzie to sit still and watch it with her. Sam sat in his recliner and watched with them, until Kenzie fell asleep around eight. The movie was almost over by then, and he and Indie started watching another one.

It was almost nine PM when his phone rang, and Sam pulled it out to see Ingersoll's number on the display. "Yes," he said, answering instantly.

"Mr. Prichard, I've made some calls and located the package you were asking about, and I've been assured that it's in perfect condition. However, there is a hitch in getting it to you, and this is where the contingency I mentioned earlier comes into play."

Sam sighed. "What do you need?" he asked.

Ingersoll spoke softly. "Listen carefully, for I have to be cautious how I say these things. The package was brought to us by a certain deliveryman, and that deliveryman then took another package from us, to deliver elsewhere. Are you with me so far?"

Sam knew what he was saying: that when Rice dropped off his daughter, he took a package of drugs or money or something that he was supposed to take to another city. "Yes, I am."

"Good. That deliveryman was supposed to make a delivery at another location, but our package has not arrived. We need to recover it, Mr. Prichard, and as quickly as we can. Since we have lost track of that deliveryman, we would like to engage you to locate and retrieve our package. In return, we will see to it that the package you are looking for is returned to you."

Sam sat up straight. "So, if I can find the 'deliveryman' that took your package and get it back for you, then you'll let me have the original package? How do I know you'll come through?"

"Mr. Prichard, despite what you may think, we are men of our word. To prove that to you, we're going to do the one thing you would never expect of us. We're going to pay in advance. The package you want will be delivered to you, in good condition, within the hour, and we are relinquishing all claim to it. All we ask is that you prove as resourceful in locating our missing package as you did in tracking this one."

Sam's eyes went wide. "I can assure you, sir, I will do my best. And—thank you."

Ingersoll laughed. "I doubt you want to thank me, Mr. Prichard. There will undoubtedly be parts of this arrangement that you will not like; just remember that you agreed to lose certain information, and we will remember not to have anything bad happen to you or the young lady staying with you."

The line went dead.

Sam stared at the phone for a long moment.

"Sam?" Indie asked. "You okay?"

"That was the man I talked to earlier today. He has just agreed to return Cassie to me, tonight, within the hour, but the price for this is that I have to find Allen Rice for them and get back whatever it was that he took."

She was staring at him. "Wait a minute, they're giving her back? Just like that? Sam, that doesn't make sense."

"I know," he said, nodding. "They're only doing it to put me in the position of owing them, so I'll feel more obligated to find Rice."

"And what happens to him once you find him?"

Sam was wondering the same thing, but his concern for Rice was overshadowed by his concern over the implied threat that ended the call. Ingersoll knew about Indie, at least that she was staying with him. If he'd known that she was the means by which Sam was acquiring his information, Sam suspected they would have already demanded her involvement, so he probably thought she was nothing but a girlfriend; a romantic involvement would make it likely that Sam would be protective of her, so that would be another level of leverage they had on him. Okay, good, let them think that.

"Indie, whoever the people are that guy is working for, they know you're staying here, and hinted that if I don't do what they want, something bad could happen to you. I think they believe you're my girlfriend, and I'd really prefer they not find out what you can do, information-wise, you follow me?"

He could see the wheels spinning in her head, but it was less than two seconds before she smiled sweetly, and said, "I'm with you, babe. All part of the job, right, still no strings, though?"

It was Sam's turn to run her words through the Enigma Machine, and then he grinned. "Still no strings. But let's let anyone watching think we're getting pretty serious, okay?"

Indie giggled. "Okay, but I'm gonna lay it on thick whenever anyone's lookin', so you better have some good self-control. Now, what about Cassie? When is she supposed to be coming home?"

"All he said was 'within the hour.' Could be any time, I guess, and I don't know if she'll be dropped off at home, or here, or where. We'll just have to wait and see." He got up and hobbled without the cane to the front door, looked out through the window, and then said, "Holy Geez..." as he snatched the door open.

Indie glanced at Kenzie, still sound asleep on the couch, and then ran over to stand beside Sam. Two men were walking up to his front porch, and both were dressed in black, SWAT-like uniforms, but neither appeared to be armed. One of them was carrying what Sam first thought was the body of Cassie Rice, and he was just about to reach for the Glock that was still on his hip when the other one put a finger to his lips and whispered, "Shh. We were told not to wake her if possible. You're Mr. Prichard?"

Sam nodded. "Yeah; she's really okay?"

The guy actually grinned. "She's fine, other than a serious sugar crash. We were told to take her out for ice cream on her way home, and let her have all she wanted, then wait 'til she passed out to bring her to you." He reached slowly into a pocket on the leg of his combat trousers and extracted an envelope, then held it out to Sam. "I was also told to give this to you." Sam took it and glanced at it, but only put it into his own pocket.

The men were on the porch by this time, and Sam moved aside to let them bring the sleeping girl in. The guy holding her laid her down on the couch, on the opposite end from Kenzie, then smiled at Sam.

"We're just hired security," he said, "and our employers told us to tell you that all we did was babysit and make sure the little princess there was safe and got whatever she needed."

"We're paid off, now," said the other one, "and we won't be working for them again, so if you need anything..." He handed Sam a card that read *Darkhouse Security Services.* "I'm Terry Darkhouse. Call anytime. Seems you shook those guys up, and that isn't easy to do."

The two men walked out and down to the car that Sam hadn't even noticed until that moment, got into it and drove away. He watched them go, then turned around to look at the sleeping girl.

Indie was kneeling beside her, and had a hand on her forehead. "Hey, sweetie," she said. "Hey, wake up." Cassie moaned for a moment, then stretched and finally opened her eyes. She looked at Indie and frowned.

"Who are you?" she asked, and then she saw Sam. "Are you the man they said was gonna take me home?"

Indie smiled and beat him to it. "That's him, honey," she said. "That's him."

Sam took out his phone and dialed Sandy Ward's number. "Mrs. Ward? Sam. I think you should come down here; your granddaughter is sitting on my couch, and wants to go home."

6

Since Cassie had been returned unharmed, as promised, and all she knew was that her father had told her he arranged for her to have some fun for a few days, which she did—she'd been to every theme park and fun spot within a hundred miles, always with her two black-clad escorts—it was decided to keep her return quiet. Her grandmother took her home, and Sam told Mrs. Ward that he didn't think they'd be seeing Rice for a long time, if ever again. The woman thanked him over and over, insisting that she could make payments to him, but Sam told her it was all just part of the neighborhood swap, and to let it go.

Indie held his hand and smiled as they walked away. "Neighborhood swap?" she asked.

He nodded and closed the door, then let go of her hand. "Long story. When I was first hurt, some of the neighbors started coming over and helping out with things, like the lawn and such. They wouldn't let me pay them, but I'm a good mechanic, so when one of 'em needed some work on his car, I was able to help him out. It sort of snowballed from there, but now we all help out whenever we can, and everyone benefits."

"I see. So, now, you're gonna be the neighborhood private eye, right?"

Sam sighed as he sat down in his recliner. "Probably," he said. "But not 'til I find Allen Rice. They held up their end, I'm gonna hold up mine."

Kenzie had wakened when Cassie and Mrs. Ward were there, but it was nearing midnight and she was dozing again. Indie looked down at her and said, "About bedtime, I think, don't you?"

He nodded. "Yeah, I'm ready to crash. I'll see you in the morning, okay?"

"Sure. Hey, question: you found her, so is that the end of the job for me?"

Sam stopped and turned to look at her. "I thought we agreed you were staying on as housekeeper?"

Indie smiled. "We did," she said. "I just wanted to be sure. And you're gonna need me to find Rice, right?"

"Yep. Now go get the little one to bed, and yourself, too. Scat!"

Indie giggled as she carried Kenzie up the stairs, and Sam smiled as he watched her go. He had to admit that it was a very pleasant view.

He went to his room and put the Glock into the drawer of his nightstand, then took out the envelope the men had given him. He looked it over carefully, but could find no sign of wires or trigger mechanisms that might indicate a letter bomb, so he slowly slid a thumb under the flap and opened it. There were papers inside, and a stack of hundred-dollar bills. He dumped the contents out onto his bed.

He glanced at the money—ten thousand dollars—but let it lie there as he picked up a typed sheet of paper. It read:

Mr. Prichard,

Despite your history with the police and the obvious conflict that may cause you with our company, we are not quite as evil as you assume us to be. Returning the girl to you in advance of our request for your assistance is, we hope, some evidence of that.

That being said, we do feel that you have a better chance of finding our missing package than we do, and are grateful for your assistance. The money included herein is intended as a retainer, with more to follow if you are successful. For the record, this money is from my own very legitimate business interests, which I never mingle with the other ventures of which we spoke earlier. You can accept it in good conscience.

Here is what we do know. Mr. Rice has been asking for some time to be given greater responsibility in the company; in effect, he wanted to become a regional sales manager. We did not feel he was ready for such a position, but after repeated requests, we decided to give him a small task and test him. That task was to take a small package of our merchandise to another location and deliver it, then see to its distribution and report back to us within five days. He was to bring back with him the proceeds of the entire operation. He should have been back here two days ago.

In the interest of aiding you in accomplishing your mission, we're going to give you the information we have. Allen Rice left here on Sunday morning, planning to drive to St. Louis, Missouri. His instructions were to find a Miss Caroline Baker and deliver the goods to her, then work with her as her new manager while she distributed the goods. The trip should have taken him about fifteen hours, but according to Miss Baker, he never arrived at all.

The car he was driving was one of ours, a silver 2015 Lincoln MKZ. We have checked, and it has not turned up in any accidents or incidents, so we suspect that Mr. Rice has simply absconded with our goods. We have no idea where he may have gone, so we are handing you quite a problem, but the fact that you were able to learn so much about us in such a short time indicates that you have some significant resources in gathering information. As long as those resources are working for us, rather than against us, we would like to maintain a mutually beneficial working relationship with you, and in accordance with your request, we will not ask you to do anything outside the law.

For that reason, all we ask you to do in this case is to locate either Mr. Rice or our goods. We will not ask you *to take any action, or to physically touch anything. Simply notify us of the location, and we will do the rest.*

We hope this meets with your approval, Mr. Prichard. If it does, we can assure you that we will also make our resources available to you in the future, should you ever need information that we can provide.

Incidentally, we do understand that you have friends in certain circles who are expecting you to give them some of your information. We can afford to lose some of our lower-level staff, in order to allow you to keep your relationship there in good standing. No offense will be taken if you need to give some of them up, now and then.

E.I.

Sam read it through several times. If he were reading it correctly, then as long as he kept his end of the bargain, Indie and Kenzie would be in no danger. He could do that, he knew, simply by not giving Dan and the DEA all of the information he had. There was still plenty he could give them, in the "lower-level staff" the letter spoke of, but by leaving out names like Ingersoll's, he could eliminate any risk to Indie and her daughter, thereby also eliminating the need to pretend she was his girlfriend.

Sam wasn't sure he liked that.

When morning came, he woke to find Indie and Kenzie up and in the kitchen again. There were pancakes and sausage cooking, and he found his coffee freshly poured and waiting on the table.

"Good morning, ladies," he said cheerfully.

"Mornin', Sam!" said Kenzie, and Sam smiled as he tickled her chin. Indie laughed and said, "Morning! Hope you like pancakes!"

"I like food!" he said. "I'll eat anything that don't eat me first, and a few things that would!"

She slid a plate of two big pancakes and a couple of sausage links in front of him, and a single pancake and link in front of Kenzie. Sam reached for the butter and offered some to Kenzie, who nodded excitedly, so he slathered some onto her pancake before doing the same to his own, then waited for Indie to join them and supervise the syrup. Kenzie said grace, and they all said, "Amen!"

"I was thinking," Sam said, "that since you're going to be staying a while, we need to get some furniture for Kenzie and set her up a room, upstairs, don't you think?"

Indie froze, and just looked at him. "Um—that'd be great, Sam, but it'd probably cost a lot, too, wouldn't it? I don't want you to go to any extra expense."

He shrugged. "It won't cost that much, and since we need to keep people thinking we're an item, it would be in character. I've got some cash saved up, and you can take it and go to the Furniture Discount Warehouse, or whatever it's called. Get her a bed of her own, and dressers, that sort of stuff."

Indie looked at him for a moment, then turned to Kenzie. "You hear that, baby? You want your own bedroom?"

Kenzie lit up like a light bulb, and Sam grinned from ear to ear. They talked all through breakfast about the kind of canopy bed Kenzie would like to have, and what Disney characters were her favorites for decorating her new room. Sam wondered if this was anything like what it would have felt like if he'd had a family of his own, and finally decided that he didn't care. He was just going to enjoy it while he could.

There was no doubt in his mind that Indie and Kenzie would move along, someday. One of the things he knew very well was that nothing lasts forever, not in this world, and he would make sure he was prepared for the heartaches that would come when that day arrived. For now, though, he would enjoy the game, the pretense that they were his family, that Indie was his girl.

When they were done eating, Indie got Kenzie settled into the living room with some educational programs for children, and she and Sam went to the dining room to get back on the computer.

"Okay, so this morning I thought about how to track Rice, and put Herman to going through all of his emails and other communications to find where he's hiding. The IP address he logs into his email from is out of a little place called Harrison, Arkansas, and so I started checking hotels there, going into some of the back doors of the bigger chain hotels. There's a Super 8 motel in Harrison that uses wifi through that IP address, and there's an Allen Rice registered there since last Sunday night."

Sam shook his head. "This idiot actually used his own name to get a hotel? I'm surprised the company couldn't find him on their own."

"Well, they probably could have if he'd used a credit card, but as far as I can tell, he doesn't even have one. He paid cash for the room for one night, and has been paying each day to stay over."

Sam sucked on his bottom lip for a moment. "Something isn't making sense to me, here. He apparently headed for St. Louis, just like he was supposed to, but then took a detour into Arkansas. There, he got a hotel room and has been just staying there, day after day, without calling in once to try to get himself out of trouble. Is he really that stupid?"

"Either that, or there's something going on that isn't obvious to us or them. I mean, why would he blow the deal he's been trying to get? He finally got his shot, it doesn't make sense he'd just throw it all away without a reason."

Sam sat there and thought about it, but couldn't come up with a better explanation than stupidity, so he gave up. "Okay. Well, I'd probably better go there and make sure this is really him, before I give them the address. If I head out this morning, I can be there by tonight, make sure it's him, and then keep him in sight while they come and do whatever they're gonna do."

Indie looked at him. "And what if what they do is kill him?"

"I've considered that," Sam said, "and the truth is, if he was stupid enough to scam these kind of people, then he's brought that down on himself. If I hand him over, then it may be faster, but sooner or later they're gonna find him, and it's gonna happen. I can either stand up to them and try to be a hero and get us all killed, or I can do what I'm hired to do and let him deal with the consequences of his actions. If it comes down to a choice between him getting hurt or you and Kenzie getting hurt, then it's gonna be him. End of story."

She stared at him for a moment, then nodded. "Okay," she said. "I just don't want you to get to feeling later like our being here forced you to do something you didn't want to do."

Sam laughed. "I'll tell you a little secret about me. No one, no matter how they complain that someone made them do something, or that they got trapped into doing something, no one ever does anything they don't want to do. The difference between me and most people is that I *know* I don't do anything I don't want to do! This guy bought his own ticket to hell, Indie, I didn't buy it for him. It's his ride, and his fault he's got to take it."

Indie smiled. "Okay. You just stay in close touch with me, okay? I'm gonna be worried about you."

Sam grinned. "I'm tougher than I look, I promise you," he said. "You don't have to worry about me."

She winked at him. "Worrying is a girlfriend's prerogative, Sam, and don't you forget it!"

Sam went to his room and began packing a few things to take along. He didn't anticipate being gone more than a couple of days, so he packed enough clothes for an overnight trip, then clipped the Glock onto his belt and slipped the three extra clips into his bag. When he was ready, he picked up the stack of hundreds and broke the band, peeling off ten of them and putting the rest into his pocket. He went out to where Indie was still sitting at the dining table.

"Here," he said, and handed her the ten hundred-dollar bills. "That's a thousand, and it ought to be enough to get the bedroom setup you want. You can use what's left over to get blankets and sheets and stuff, and if you need more, we'll do that when I get back, okay?"

Indie smiled up at him. "Okay. You know, you don't have to do this, right? Me and Kenzie can sleep in the same room, it's no big deal."

He looked over to where Kenzie was enthralled by Dora the Explorer, and nodded toward her. "You've done pretty good by her under the circumstances you've had to deal with, Indie, but a child needs some kind of stability and individuality in her life. Since you've agreed to stay here and work for me for a while, we might as well let her get started on that, don't you think? Giving her a bedroom isn't hurting me any, and it's not like I've got a woman waiting for me to propose or anything; the extra rooms up there'll be empty for a long time if you don't use one of 'em for Kenzie, so why not? It'll give you time to find a real job, the kind you want, and to get on your feet again."

She stood up and looked him in the eye for moment, staring up at his six foot one from her "five foot nothing," as he'd put it, then reached up and grabbed the sides of his face and pulled him down for a kiss. It wasn't a passionate kiss, it was just a kiss, but there was a hint in it that there could be more, if he played his cards right.

"Thank you," she said, and let him go.

Sam had admitted to himself months earlier that the Vette was finished, but he hadn't taken it out for a drive yet. As he walked out the front door—after a tearful goodbye from Kenzie, who was afraid he might not come back—he suddenly decided the van just wasn't the way he wanted to go, so he hit the button on his key fob and opened the garage door. Indie had followed him out and was watching as it rolled up, and her eyes bugged out when she saw what was hidden inside.

"Holy cow," she said, "that is beautiful! What is it?"

"Nineteen sixty-nine Corvette Stingray," Sam said. "I bought it a few years ago when it was seized in a drug deal, and been rebuilding it ever since. It's been done for a few months, but I haven't had a reason to take her out, 'til now." He went to the car and opened the door, tossing his bag inside before climbing in. He sat there for a moment, then put the key into the ignition and fired up the aluminum 427-cubic-inch engine known as the ZL1.

The rumble that came from the twin factory-side exhaust pipes was enough to make the windows rattle in the house, and when he eased the clutch out, the car slid forward like a shark moving toward a swimmer. Indie was still staring, and when Sam stopped it right in front of her and powered down the passenger window, she leaned in and said, "Remind me that when you get back, you're taking me for a ride in this thing!"

He laughed. "Sounds like a date!"

Indie looked around the interior of the car and then back into his eyes. "It might be," she said, and then turned and let him watch her wiggle her way back into the house. She got inside and looked at her daughter, who was still watching TV, and said, "Sweetie—it might be just barely possible that we've found the nicest guy there is! How would you feel about having Sam for a Daddy?"

Kenzie, who Indie had thought wasn't listening, spun around and said, "Yeah! Sam's gonna be my Daddy! Yay!"

Uh-oh, Indie thought. *I hope she forgets that before he gets home!*

Sam got onto I-70 at the Steel Street ramp and let the Vette have its head. He was cruising at eighty before he even realized it, and just enjoyed the feel of the powerful car beneath him. The road slid by like water over a dam, and he let himself think through all that had happened in the past few days.

Sam had thought his working days were over, and he'd certainly never thought he'd be doing any kind of investigative work again. When Mrs. Ward had come to him about Cassie, his instinct was to consider it beyond his ability to find the girl, but in essence, he had done just that. She was home safe because he'd done what had to be done.

Of course, a lot of that was attributable to Indie. It was her skills with computers that made it possible for him to learn the things he was able to use as leverage, and so he owed a lot to her, too. A part of him thought that they made a great team, and he had already decided to offer her more pay to help with any further cases he might get. That might get her to stay longer, anyway, and he was ready to admit to himself that he really liked having her and Kenzie around. They'd been with him less than two whole days, and it already felt like they just belonged there with him.

On the other hand, Sam wasn't the type to jump in too fast. He'd want to go slow, even though he got the feeling that Indie was interested in letting the relationship grow, too. The kiss she'd given him—that had come out of nowhere, but he'd certainly enjoyed it! Heck, he'd love to go right back there and kiss her again!

Down, boy, he said to himself. He'd already realized

that Indie was very pretty, but watching her go up the stairs the night before had made him admit that he found her sexy as could be, too. That little wiggle of hers was something few men could ever fail to admire, and he wasn't one of them! He could watch that all day long, but it only led to thoughts of other things that he'd promised not to try, so he made himself behave as long as she was around.

The miles were passing, and it wasn't long before he was in Kansas. I-70 took him to Kansas City, and his GPS told him that he'd go south there onto I-49. He had a few hours of Kansas flatland ahead, though, so he cruised along, only stopping for gas, and once for a sandwich.

Back in Denver, Indie had googled all the local discount furniture places, and decided to go shopping. She cleaned Kenzie up and dressed her, and the two of them got into her car and headed for the first one on her list.

They walked into the store, and a salesman spotted them instantly, but he seemed more interested in hitting on her than finding the things she wanted to see. After about fifteen minutes, she said she'd forgotten something at home and would be back, then drove off to the next store. That one was more rewarding, and the sales lady there was happy to help her find a perfect bedroom suite for Kenzie, and even discounted it more when she found out that Indie was paying cash! She got everything she wanted for less than five hundred, and was delighted!

Then it was off to the mall and the stores that sold bedding for kids. Kenzie ended up with Frozen-themed bedding from the Disney store, and a Dora-themed set from another one. They bought appliques to put up around the walls, and pictures of some of Kenzie's favorite characters to hang around the room, and Indie still had enough left to buy Kenzie some toys and even a little table and chair set that the two of them fell in love with. When she rang it all up and was stuffing it into her car, she hoped Sam wouldn't mind the extras, but she somehow had the feeling that he would be okay with it.

She got everything in the car, even though the table was stuffed into the back seat next to Kenzie, and started for home. She thought about the fact that she'd have the big house to herself for the night, and that made her feel a bit lonely. Sam was a very nice guy, and she had already come to realize that she was very attracted to him, but she wasn't sure how he felt about her. Okay, yeah, she could tell he thought she was cute, and she knew he was watching her go up the stairs the night before, which gave her a tingle if she was going to be honest, but was he actually interested in *her*, or just in her femaleness? He was a man, after all, so she needed to be careful not to give him the wrong signals, and not to read his wrong, either.

She got home and was unloading her purchases when Anita Mitchell came down to see if Kenzie wanted to come over and play for a while. Kenzie certainly did, so Indie had the rest of the afternoon to start putting things together, and when the furniture store's delivery truck showed up at three, the guys driving it were thrilled to help her get everything set up.

Sam's gonna be amazed at how much I got, she thought, *and I bet he likes it all, too. Maybe it'll show him I'm worth his notice...*

She shut down that train of thought, instantly.

Sam wondered if there was ever a place as boring and flat as Kansas. Holy cow, he hadn't seen anything taller than a small tree in two hundred miles! He'd passed Hays, Salina, Abilene, Junction City, and Topeka, and was coming up on Kansas City, but still, it was almost nothing but flatland. How could anyone live there?

He checked his GPS and got ready to make the turn onto 49. He'd have to follow that down to a town called Fayetteville, Arkansas, where he'd get onto Highway 412, a back road if he ever saw one! That would be the one to take him to Harrison, where Allen Rice was hiding out.

He checked the time and saw that it was getting close to five, so he called Indie just to see how she was doing. A part of him was feeling bad for not telling her she didn't have to play the girlfriend after all, but another part wanted to keep it going as long as possible. When she answered, he decided to see how quick she was.

"Hey, Baby, how's it going?" he asked, a smile evident in his voice.

"Well, hi there, Darlin'!" she came back. "It's goin'

good, here, how's the road trip?"

"It's long and boring. I've come to the conclusion that Kansas is the place God created for people who are too afraid of life to live in the mountains! There is nothing in Kansas taller than a rabbit!"

Indie laughed, and Sam realized that he liked hearing her laugh. "Well, I went shopping, like you told me to do," she said, "and I did really good. I got everything I needed to set up her bedroom, and I hope it's okay, but I kinda bought her some toys and stuff, too."

Sam grinned. "That's fine, and now that you mention it, I should probably buy her something while I'm out, too. I think she'd liked to know I was thinking of her, so if I bring her back a toy or something..."

"She loves stuffed animals," Indie said. "Any kind, she just loves them!"

"I'll remember that!"

They were both quiet for a moment, and then they both tried to speak at once.

"So, I was thinking..."

"Indie, I was wondering...okay, you go first."

"No, you go on, I can wait," Indie said.

"Well—I was just gonna ask, does it bother you, having to pretend we're, y'know, an item?"

She hesitated for a moment, and Sam cringed, afraid of what she was about to say, but then she said, "No, I don't mind. I mean, you're a good-lookin' guy, so we probably look nice together, y'know, and you're so good to me and Kenzie. I mean, it wouldn't bother me, y'know, if we had to—if we had to keep it up for a while, y'know?"

Sam was smiling and nodding into the phone. "Okay, good, cause I think maybe, if you're okay with it, I think maybe we should keep it this way for a while, maybe even quite a while, just to be safe, you know, and so when I get back, maybe we can start going out, like on dates, you know?"

Indie swallowed hard. "Yeah, that'd probably be a good idea, y'know, let everyone see us out like we're really boyfriend and girlfriend, y'know."

They kept assuring each other that it was a good idea for a few more minutes, and then Sam's phone beeped an incoming call. He said goodbye, and switched over.

"Hello?"

"Hey, Stranger," said Dan Jacobs. "Anything good goin' on over there?"

"Well, some things," Sam said. "I found the girl, and got her home last night, but it's led to a mess. In return for getting her back, I've got to find Allen Rice, who is hiding in some little town in Arkansas. I'm headed there now."

"Geez, Arkansas? Is that a real place?"

"Yeah, it's real," Sam laughed. "Listen, I haven't forgotten about you. I'm putting together some info you're gonna find useful, but I'm afraid it's mostly just street scum."

"Hey, every little bit helps! If I can make a few good busts, I have a chance of getting a promotion one of these days, and I could use the pay raise that would come with it!"

Sam smiled. Dan was always complaining about his pay, even though he lived alone and had no real expenses. "I'll see what I can do to speed that up for you!"

"Okay, good. You be careful in Arkansas, I've heard stories about those rednecks out there!"

They hung up, and Sam saw his exit ahead. He was in Missouri, and it was time to go south to redneck land. He followed 49 all the way to Fayetteville, Arkansas, passing through Bentonville (the Home of Wal-Mart) on the way. He found his exit for US 412, and followed it, moving through small hills and vales that were known locally as The Ozark Mountains.

How anyone could call these speed bumps mountains is beyond me, he thought. The road was curvy and wound up and down, but it was decent and well maintained, so he was making good time.

It was getting late, nearing eleven in the evening, and he hadn't stopped for several hours. He spotted a big gas station and store in a little town called Marble that was barely more than a wide spot in the road, and pulled in to gas up. The store sported a small restaurant, and he bought some chicken strips to eat on the way.

"That be all for you?" the counter girl asked as he paid for his gas and purchases.

"That'll be it. Can you tell me how much farther it is to Harrison?"

She nodded. "Oh, yeah, Harrison's about another forty-five minutes or an hour ahead. You're almost there."

He got back on the road and let the Vette cruise again, and sure enough, he found Harrison right where she'd said he would. He rolled into town past the Wal-Mart and car lots and banks, and spotted the Super 8 Hotel, then pulled in and got a room.

7

Sam got up at six the next morning and wandered out to the lobby for the free continental breakfast they'd told him about when he checked in. Waffles sounded good, and they had the machine there that made them fresh on the spot. He got himself a cup of coffee, then started his waffle, and was standing beside the counter waiting for it when Allen Rice strolled into the breakfast room.

Rice looked nervous, Sam thought. There was something about the guy that said he was scared, and while Sam could understand that, it struck him as odd that Rice was hanging out in some little redneck town in the middle of nowhere. He should have been in some other part of the world. Sam didn't know how much money Rice may have taken off with, or how much value the drugs he took may have had, but if it was worth leaving his daughter as collateral, it was probably a substantial amount. Surely it could have gotten him somewhere further and more anonymous than Harrison, Arkansas!

All Sam knew at the moment, though, was that he had confirmed the location of Rice, and that meant his job was almost done.

The waffle iron went *ding*, which meant his waffle was done. He got it out of the machine and onto a plate, then smothered it in butter and syrup and carried it to one of the little tables. He sat down as Rice began making a waffle of his own.

Rice sat at the table beside his, and began to eat hunkered down over the plate as if he was afraid someone was going to steal his breakfast away. Sam didn't understand why, but something about the way Rice was acting was bothering him, and if there was one thing Sam couldn't take, it was not understanding something.

"Good waffles, here, aren't they?" he said, before he even realized he was going to speak.

Rice looked up at him and grunted something that may have been agreement, then turned his eyes back down to his plate. A second later, he jumped as his cell phone rang, and he snatched it out and answered in a whisper.

"Hello?" he said softly into the phone. "Hey, Babe, thanks for calling me back. I didn't know who else to call."

He listened for a few moments, and Sam strained to hear any of what the caller was saying, but it wasn't loud enough. He could tell it was a woman's voice, and he suspected it was the girlfriend he'd met at Rice's house.

"I don't know what to do," Rice was saying. "I've waited here for most of a week, now, and no one has come like they said. I'm gettin' scared, Babe. This is too weird, but when I call 'em, no one answers. It's like they put me out here to be a bait, or something, but I don't know what for."

Sam was listening to the words, but he was also listening to the voice Rice was using, and it was one that was full of fear and worry. The skin on the back of Sam's neck was prickling, and something told him that things were not right, here.

"If I don't hear something by tomorrow," Rice said into the phone, "I'm comin' home. They can take this job and shove it. I don't want no part of this. They can give me Cassie back, I'll give their stuff back, and I'll just go on my way and they can go theirs!" He listened again for a moment, then sighed. "Okay, Babe, well, if that guy comes back, you go ahead and call me and let me talk to him. This is just gettin' too weird, like I said." He ended the call and put the phone back into his pocket.

Sam pretended not to have heard anything, finishing his waffle like everything was fine. He drank his coffee and then refilled his cup, trying to wait until Rice was done. He wanted to talk to the man, but not here where the desk clerk could hear everything said.

His patience was rewarded a moment later, as Rice threw his plate and cup away and started toward the elevator. Sam caught up to him and tapped him on the arm just before he pushed the button.

"Mr. Rice, I think we need to talk," he said, and Rice immediately spun to face him. He threw his back against the wall behind him and stared at Sam, the fear evident in his face.

"Are you gonna kill me?" he asked in a quavering voice.

"Not intentionally," Sam said. "Let's go to my room and talk, shall we? I promise I'm not going to hurt you. And if that was Carly you were talking to, then I'm probably the guy who came to talk to her that she told you about. The one asking about Cassie?"

Rice swallowed. "Why are you here? How did you find me?"

"I'm a private eye, and I'm very good at what I do," Sam said. "We can talk in my room. Right now I just want to find out why you're here, and why certain people are looking for you so hard."

Rice stared at him for a moment, then nodded, and Sam pointed down the hall to his room. Because of his cane, the clerk the night before had given him a ground floor room, and they slipped inside and shut the door.

"Have a seat," Sam said, and Rice took one of the chairs at the table across from the bed. Sam sat in the other and looked at him. "I couldn't help overhearing your phone call a bit ago, and I gotta tell you, something is sounding pretty fishy to me. See, I was hired first to find your daughter, by her grandmother; that led me to tracking you down, and I found out about your deal with the Company, the one where they held your daughter for security. That made me track down one of the owners of the Company, and..."

Rice's eyes went wide. "You know who they are?" he asked in panic-stricken tones. "Man, they'll kill anyone who knows who they are! That's one of the first things they tell us: if we ever try to find out who they are, we're dead!"

Sam held out a hand to calm him down. "Relax; all I know is one of them, and he and I have an agreement. I don't mess with him, and he won't mess with me. In fact, it was them who hired me to come and track you down. According to what they told me, they think you took off with a lot of their dope or money, or both, and I think they're out for your blood."

Rice stared at him. "They think I—oh, God, I'm dead! I'm dead! Did they follow you here? Did they send you to kill me? I'm dead, I'm just dead!"

"Calm down and talk to me," Sam said forcefully. "If there's a legitimate reason why you're here instead of in St. Louis or Denver, then maybe I can find a way to keep you alive. The way I got it, you were supposed to take a load of merchandise to St. Louis and give it to a woman named Baker. Is that what you were told?"

Rice nodded slowly. "Yes, at first, but then when I was on the road, they called and told me to go and hide somewhere, instead. They said someone was after me, and they didn't want me to get caught with it, so I should go somewhere no one would look for me and hide until they called, but I been here for days and no one's called!"

"Okay, who called and told you that? Was it the same one who sent you to St. Louis?"

Rice nodded. "Yeah, I don't know his name or nothin'. He's my district leader. Usually we only talk on email, but when you're a crew leader, you get a phone so they can talk to you that way." He held out the cell phone he'd been using earlier. "He called me when I hit Kansas City and told me to go somewhere else and hide 'til he calls me back. I turned off and followed a bunch of different roads 'til I got too tired to keep going, and stopped here."

Sam was thinking, and not liking the ideas that were going through his mind. The way he saw it, there were only three possibilities:

First, someone was setting Rice up for a fall by sending him into the wind with a lot of the Company's value, and that someone was planning to take that value for himself. That plan almost certainly involved killing Rice in the process.

Second, someone was setting Sam up. He had been hired to find Rice, but someone probably already knew right where he was, and a hit team could be waiting to strike at any moment. If it did, and Rice were killed, Sam would be the most likely suspect.

Third, Rice was set up, but whoever was behind it really did lose track of him. They hired Sam to find him, and would have to eliminate both of them once the job was done.

None of the options held much appeal for Sam, but he had to choose the most likely one, and fast. That would dictate his next move, and if it was the wrong one, then he and Rice, and maybe even Indie and Kenzie, were going to end up dead.

"Rice, tell me this: do you still have whatever it is they gave you? All of it?"

Rice smiled from ear to ear. "You bet your ass, I do! No way was I letting it out of my sight!"

Sam breathed a small sigh of relief. That was one part of the problem out of the way. "Good. Now, tell me about the man you talked to on the phone. What does he sound like?"

Rice looked at him, not comprehending. "Sound like? I dunno, he sounds like a guy from the South, I guess. Got a Southern-type accent, know what I mean? Like he's from Texas or somewhere like that."

Okay, Sam thought, *that's not Ingersoll. He's more the city-tough-guy type, pretending to be a society gentleman.* "Sit tight," he said to Rice. "I've gotta make a phone call, and you don't want this guy to know you're here, not yet. Be as quiet as you possibly can, but I'm gonna let you hear his voice, and all I want you to do is nod or shake your head, to tell me if it's the voice you know. Got that?"

Rice nodded. "Yeah, I got it. I won't make a sound!"

Sam took out his phone and hit the button to dial Ingersoll's phone. As he expected, it was answered almost immediately.

"Mr. Prichard," the voice said, "are you calling to give me good news already?"

Sam held the phone so Rice could hear the voice on the other end, and watched Rice's face. When the man shook his head calmly, indicating that he did not know Ingersoll's voice, Sam relaxed a bit.

"Well, I'm not so sure it's good news, but I've got something. I have located your missing package, and its deliveryman, but it appears to me that you've got a problem somewhere at your end. The delivery was rerouted by whoever originally sent the package on its way, and the deliveryman was told to wait for new instructions."

Ingersoll was silent for several seconds. "Mr. Prichard, do you have reason to believe this is actually true?"

"I'm afraid I do, sir. I'm here with the deliveryman now, who assures me your package is present and intact, and he's been waiting here for those new instructions for several days. Long enough that even he's begun to get suspicious, but he didn't know whom to call."

More silence for another ten seconds. "I see. Well, it appears that I do have a problem. However, you have done your job, so if you wish you can walk away now and I'll forward the additional fee I mentioned in my letter— but if you're willing, I think I could stand to employ you a bit longer."

Sam smiled. "What do you have in mind?" he asked.

"I should like for that deliveryman to return to Denver safely, and I suspect that there may be someone who is not going to want that to happen, don't you? I'm afraid I made an error in judgment, Mr. Prichard, and that I must now confess it to you; the person of whom we are speaking was made aware of our arrangement, and has almost certainly been following you. I think that if you accept this new assignment, you should probably take that deliveryman and his package and vacate your location within the next few minutes."

Sam caught on instantly; whoever had sent Rice on this wild mission was almost certainly following him, and most likely was watching the hotel at that moment. They'd be out to get Rice and his package, and wouldn't care who got in the way.

"Wait a minute," Sam said. "If this is the person who sent the original shipment, then why wouldn't he know where the deliveryman is? He called him by phone to tell him to divert, but he's never called him back. Are you sure we're talking about the same one?"

"I'm afraid we are, and the reason your deliveryman was lost is very simple; the phone the deliveryman has is one of thousands that we use and then throw away once they've served their purpose. It was programmed for this one shipment only, and its number entered into only the phone of the person sending it out. Unfortunately, that phone suffered a mishap the other evening, and fell into a bathtub. By the time it was dried out, its memory was completely wiped, and the shipper no longer has the deliveryman's number. He does, however, know what you are driving, and he and his helpers have been following you since you left yesterday morning. Once again, Mr. Prichard, I would not waste any time in getting away from where you are. Good luck."

The line went dead. Sam looked at Rice and knew that he didn't have time to explain everything.

"Where is the package, Mr. Rice?" he demanded. He'd already made such an impression that Rice didn't hesitate.

"I told you, I never let it out of my sight," Rice said. "It's right here!" He reached into a pocket and produced a small, square bottle.

Sam stared. "That's it? What on earth is in it?"

Rice shrugged his shoulders. "I don't have a clue, but whatever it is, it must be pretty strong stuff. I mean, they'd have to cut it thousands of times to do any good with it, right?"

Sam reached out and took the bottle from Rice's hand and just looked at it for a moment. The top was sealed with some sort of glue-like substance. "You haven't tried to open it, have you?"

"Lord, No!" Rice said. "That's one of the things they told me. It's so strong that if I even smell it, it would probably kill me! I'm not about to touch that cap!"

Sam hefted it. It wasn't glass, he thought, but more of a heavy plastic. If it was that concentrated, that was probably a good thing. He handed it back to Rice.

"Okay, here's the deal. It looks to me like someone set you up. The guy who sent you out with this stuff is also the one who wanted you to take it and hide, but then he dropped his phone into the tub and lost your number. When I came along and was able to track your daughter to them, the guy I talked to decided to hire me to try to find you. The one who sent you out, however, he may have followed me after all, and if so, then he's probably gonna try to kill you and take that from you. My pal on the phone has asked me to try to keep you alive and get you back to Denver with it. The only way I can do that is if we leave, like right now."

Rice stared at him. "Um—okay, let me go get my..."

"No, I mean, we leave right now! My car is parked right outside that window, and that's how we're going out of here. We don't have time for you to go get anything, let's go, now!" He moved past Rice and threw open the window, then kicked the screen off of it. He stuck his head out and looked around for a moment, didn't see anyone watching, and said, "Come on, let's go," before climbing over the sill and stepping onto the grass. Three quick steps took him to the driver's door of the Vette, and Rice was suddenly at the passenger door.

Sam unlocked the driver's door and got in, then reached across and popped open the passenger door. Rice slid into the seat, and Sam told him to get low and stay that way, then backed out of his parking spot and headed toward the main street out in front of the place. He reached down and took the Glock from its holster and laid it in his lap for safety, then turned left and headed north on US 65.

He glanced into the rear-view mirror and started to congratulate himself on making a clean escape, but then he saw two cars come fishtailing out of the hotel's parking lot. "They've seen us," he said, and downshifted the Vette into second gear, flooring it. The car took off like a rocket, and he started weaving in and out of traffic like a race driver.

The cars behind him were new Mustangs, and were every bit as powerful as the Vette, he was sure. Sam could only hope he was the better driver, and that his car was better suited to the curvy roads of northwest Arkansas. When he got to the turnoff for 412, he slammed the Vette into it at more than a hundred miles an hour, taking the curving ramp at twice the speed it was built for.

The Mustangs were right behind him, though, and they were not having any trouble keeping up as he roared up the four-lane highway. He remembered that there was a small town ahead, where the road took a sharp turn to the left, and hoped he could gain some distance on them by the time they got there.

The Vette was fast and powerful, but the other cars were newer and had more advanced components that gave them handling and power that didn't exist in sixty-nine. Fortunately, they also had computerized governors that limited their top speed, despite that power. Sam pushed the Vette as hard as he could, red-lining the tachometer as he tried for just a little more power from the big aluminum V8. He was slamming the gears up and down, doing everything he could to gain just a little more advantage in this game of automotive cat and mouse. By the time he got close to the next town, the Mustangs were barely visible in the mirrors.

The sign said "Speed Zone Ahead," and he came flying into the tiny town of Alpena, Arkansas. A post office, two gas stations and a guy who carved logs into statues with a chain saw were the only claims the town had to being noticeable, and he flew past all of them at close to a hundred and fifty. The road turned left, and he had to slow down, but he still managed to drift the turn at more than seventy miles an hour. He was over the first hill by the time the Mustangs made it to the intersection, and had opened the throttle up wide.

He grabbed his phone and called Indie.

"Hello," she said, and he started talking.

"Indie, I've got troubles! The whole thing's been a setup, but somehow I've come down on the right side of it all. I've got bad guys on my tail, chasing me right now. They want to kill Rice and take what he's got, and they'll kill me, too, if they catch us! I need back roads, a way to lose the cars chasing us, and I don't have lots of time. What can you do?"

"Oh, God, Sam, let me get on the computer! Where are you now?"

"I'm on US 412, about two miles west of Alpena, Arkansas! I need a route that'll get me off this road and get me back to Denver."

"I'm lookin', I'm lookin', hang on! Okay, about nine miles ahead, you've got a road going north, it's State Highway 103. If you take that right turn, then go straight when you come to a little town called Rudd, that's a shortcut to another road, Highway 21. That'll take you to Berryville, and there's a dozen ways out of there. Those roads have lots of curves, be careful!"

Sam laughed. "Don't worry, Babe," he said, "this car was built for curves. I can handle it! I'll call you later, when I'm on a safer road!"

He ended the call and pushed the Vette, going for every bit of power he could pull out of it to keep distance between him and the two Mustangs. He told his phone to call up GPS and find the way to Berryville, and a moment later it told him he'd be turning right in two miles.

He glanced over at Rice and saw that the man was white as a sheet. He was holding onto the door with one hand and the console with the other, but his face was ashen. "Just hang on, man, I'll get you home safe!" Sam yelled over the sound of the engine and the wind.

Rice nodded and tried to grin, but didn't quite make it.

Sam slid the car into the turn for 103, and poured the power back on as he raced up the curvy road. Chicken houses and farms flashed by on either side, and then he came into a tiny little town. The main road turned hard to the right, but there was another road that went straight like Indie had said, and Sam took it, flying over a small hump in the road and then straightening out as he followed the asphalt into the hills.

He made it to Highway 21, and was sure that he'd lost the Mustangs, so he turned right and headed into Berryville. The old town was not very big, but he was able to find a way up through Missouri that would help them avoid the ones who were after them. When he was well on the way and feeling safe for the moment, he called Ingersoll again.

"Okay," he said, "I've got Rice and the package, and we're on the road. Who is it that's trying to kill us, and what the heck is this thing that can be so small and still so valuable?"

"Mr. Prichard, there are some things I'm prepared to tell you, and some that I am not. For now, you'll have to let me decide what things you need to know. The package is not one of those things. As for the person after you, I'm afraid you've identified a rebellion within our ranks, and one of our top people seems to have decided to split with us. That is who you're dealing with, but his identity is not going to do you any good. If you make it back here, then I shall be willing to meet with you and discuss some of this information, but not over the telephone. Once again, I wish you good luck, Mr. Prichard. Oh, and please tell Mr. Rice that he is not in any danger from the actual Company—provided he survives the current situation."

The line went dead again. "Damn, I hate when he does that! Just hangs up without telling me squat!"

"They're all like that," Rice said. "They only tell you what they want you to know, nothing else."

Sam looked over at him. "How many have you talked to?"

"Well, only one on the phone," he said, "but I've talked to all three of them by email. At least, I think I have. You can't really tell, that way."

"You say there's three of them? How do you know that?"

"Well, there's three districts, that's all I know for sure, so it makes sense there's only three district managers, right? That's what I mean by all three of them. I don't know how many there are over the district managers."

Sam shook his head. The Company seemed to be set up like a normal business in some ways, but it was obviously a criminal organization, and apparently ruthless. Right at the moment, all he wanted to do was survive another day. His deal with Ingersoll meant that he couldn't turn them all in, but if he could help cause the rift between the apparent leaders to get wider, then there might be an internal collapse of their system, something that would leave enough gaps for Dan and the DEA to get in and do some damage.

The road out of Arkansas wasn't very long, and they soon found themselves on US 65 once again, but this time it was going north through Branson, MO and up to Columbia. There, they would pick up I-70 again, and make their way back to Denver.

Sam thought about stopping to rent a different car, but he didn't want to leave his Vette behind and didn't want to be in something with less power if they were found. The old ZL1 was still one of the best engines ever built, and the old-style technology of the muscle car era had just proven itself superior to all the high-tech, computer-regulated power that was automatically limited in the newer machines.

He drove until he had to stop for gas, and then grabbed food for him and Rice. They ate on the fly, wolfing down their sandwiches and fries, guzzling the cokes that washed down the meal, actually starting to enjoy the ride.

Sam looked over at Rice. "So, how did you get mixed up in all this?"

The other man shrugged. "Long story, and probably one you've heard before. Me and my ex got into dealing some pot, and that led to some other stuff. She got busted and gave me up, but I fought it. It's all still going on; I got a court date in a couple months. Anyway, when I was going to my first hearing, I got approached by the Company, and they said if I wanted to work for them, they could keep me from doing any time over the bust, so I agreed, y'know? I was doing good, too, making some good money and not getting into any trouble, but I just wanted to move up, right? I felt like I could do even better, and then I got with Carly, and she liked the money I was makin' a lot, so I wanted to make even more. I started askin' about promotion opportunities, like could I run a crew, and they finally said I could if I could just handle this little job. All I had to do was take this stuff to St. Louis and give it to the crew leader there, and when I got back, I'd get my own crew. They were talkin' about giving me a crew in Vegas, man."

"And all you had to do was give them your daughter?" Sam had enough bitterness in his voice that Rice could hear it.

"It wasn't like that, man," he said. "They told me all they wanted was to hang onto her so they had reason to know I'd come back, and I was definitely gonna come back! Then this crazy crap happened, and I didn't know what to think. I couldn't get no one on the phone, and nobody was callin' me back, nothin'. I was scared, but I was gonna head back today, if I didn't hear from no one.

I wasn't gonna leave Cassie there, man, no matter what you think. I mean, I shoulda been back within two days, not a week, like this!"

Sam sneered. "Well, Cassie is safe, and luckily for you, the guy who was really in charge has at least a small streak of decency in him. Girls like her end up in some pretty messy situations when they get swapped off for dope, or used for security in deals like this. She was lucky."

Rice looked down at his hands. "Sounds like she was lucky you got involved, to me," he said. "And maybe that goes for me, too. If the man hadn't messed up his phone, I'd probably have told him where I was and I'd be dead by now. Wasn't for you, I probably still would be. They woulda found me sooner or later."

Sam couldn't argue with that, so he didn't try. He called Indie, instead.

"Oh, my God, it's about time you called me! Are you okay? I've been worried sick!"

"I'm okay, hon'," Sam said, and then realized what he'd said. "Everything okay there?"

"Yeah, we're fine, I've just been worried about you! I mean, it's not like you called me and said someone was out to kill you or anything, right? Geez!"

He talked to her for a few more minutes, then promised to call again later. When she let him off the phone, he called Ingersoll.

"Okay, we seem to have slipped the bad guys," he

said. "How are you gonna handle them on your end, or is that in the 'I don't need to know' category?"

"We're already handling it, Mr. Prichard. Our associate is fully aware that his plan has gone awry, of course, so he's decided not to return to our fair city. I don't think he'll be attempting to trouble you any longer, simply because that would bring him within our reach, and that, I promise you, is something he'll want to avoid. I doubt there's any chance he'll happen across you on the road today, anyway."

"Let's hope not," Sam said. "Now, about when we get back; you said Mr. Rice would not be in danger?"

"That is correct," Ingersoll said. "We're aware that the delay and diversion of our product was not his doing, so he is not to be held responsible. I think that any of our staff would have done the same, under similar circumstances."

"Okay, then, what do I do when we get back to Denver? Do you want me to drop him off somewhere? Let him go home? What?"

"Actually, Mr. Prichard, I think I'd like to meet you face to face, if you're willing. If you would simply call me when you're getting close to the city, I'll set up a safe meeting place and we can sit and talk like gentlemen. Would that be acceptable?"

Sam thought it over. If Ingersoll was willing to meet with him, it meant he either trusted Sam, or he planned to kill him. No matter how safe a meeting place might seem to be, a good sniper could make it a deadly trap; there would be no way to know whether it was safe or not, from Sam's point of view.

"What would we need to discuss that we can't talk about over the phone?" Sam asked.

"Mr. Prichard, let us just say that there are aspects of my business that you would find not only acceptable, but worthy of occasional support. I have found that you are a man of courage and honor, and I would like to show you why you should find me to be one, as well. We need not see entirely eye to eye in order to recognize qualities worthy of respect in each other, am I right?"

Sam grinned. "Okay, you've got my curiosity up. I'll call, and if it looks reasonably safe, I'll meet you. What about Rice?"

"You'll drop Mr. Rice off near where we will meet, and there will be people there to see to his safety. I give you my word that he will not be harmed, and he will find himself rewarded for the simple fact that he kept our product safe to the best of his ability during this fiasco. You may tell him that, if you wish."

Another dead line. "That guy says goodbye like a cat!"

Rice's eyebrows went up. "Like a cat?"

"Yeah, he just sticks his tail up into the air and leaves! Just hangs up without even saying goodbye, it's annoying! By the way, he says you're not in any trouble, and you'll be rewarded for the fact you kept the package safe the best you could in this mess. I'm supposed to drop you off with some people who will see that you're safe, and then I have to go meet him."

Rice looked over at Sam, and his face fell. "Aw, man, I'm sorry."

"Sorry? Sorry for what?"

"I told you, man, if you find out who they are, they kill you. I think he wants to meet you so he can look you in the eye before you die!"

8

It was nearing ten o'clock at night, and Indie was sitting in the living room with Kenzie when the car pulled up into the driveway. She went to the door to see who it was, and an elderly man she didn't know came walking up the steps onto the porch.

"Is Mr. Prichard here?" he asked when she opened the door.

"No, I'm afraid not," she said, and then she saw the pistol come out from behind his back and point at her face.

"Well, that's good," the old man said, "because then I'd lose the element of surprise. Let's step inside, shall we?"

Indie moved backwards, and the old man followed, his gun still up close to her face. Kenzie looked up from the TV and saw the old man, but she didn't realize what was happening. "Hi," she said.

The old man instantly smiled at Kenzie, while whispering to Indie, "I have no desire to hurt you or your daughter, my dear girl. I need to speak with Mr.

Prichard, so I want you to get him on the telephone."

She swallowed, and started to refuse, but then the old man did something that startled her. She stared at him for a moment. Then she took out her phone and punched the icon that would dial Sam's number.

He answered on the second ring. "Well, hey, good lookin'," he said.

"Sam, there's someone here who wants to talk to you," Indie said slowly, and then held the phone out to the old man. He took it and said, "Hello, Mr. Prichard. I think we have some business to discuss. And since I have something that you value, and you have something that I value, I think we should be able to come to some equitable terms, don't you?"

In the Corvette, Sam heard the southern accent and knew that this was the voice of the man who had set this whole thing in motion. He motioned for Rice to be quiet, who nodded in understanding.

"I'm listening," Sam said. "What do you have in mind?"

"It's very simple," the man said. "I want the material that you recovered from Mr. Rice. In return, I will give you the lives of these two young ladies I found in your home. This is a one-time offer, Mr. Prichard, so don't take too long to think it over."

Sam thought fast. "Look, I'm wishing I'd never even heard of this stuff, so I'm more than willing to give it up! How do you want to make the swap? Just say when, where and how, and I'm in. Those girls are a lot more important to me than this crap is."

The old man chuckled. "Oh, I'm so glad you feel that way! I thought you would, but then again, you just never know about people, nowadays. How far out are you, would you say?"

Sam knew he was only about a half hour out of town, but he wasn't going to give that away. "I'm a good two hours away, but I'm moving steadily that direction."

"Alright then, that'll give us time to get this set up. I'll call you again in about an hour, and tell you where we'll meet. Don't get any crazy ideas, now, I'd hate to have to ruin their hairstyles, but I will if you force me to. One hour, don't forget to answer!"

The line went dead, and Sam instantly called Ingersoll.

"Yes, Mr. Prichard, I assume you're getting close?"

"I'm about a half hour out, but that isn't why I'm calling. Your rogue man was just at my house, and holding my girls hostage. He wants this stuff as bad as ever, I'm guessing, and says he wants me to meet with him to trade."

Ingersoll was quiet for a long moment. "Mr. Prichard, I am truly sorry that you got involved in this. If he's got them, then I'm sure you have already figured out that he has no intention of letting them or you live, not after any of you have seen his face. That leaves us to decide how to handle the situation, for I do not want their deaths on my conscience any more than you want them on yours."

"I'm listening," Sam said, "but we better come up with something fast. I bought a little time by telling him I was two hours out. He's gonna call me back in an hour and tell me where to meet up."

Ingersoll sighed. "Well, that gives us a small advantage. I was under the impression that he was gone today, out of town, and I assumed he'd gone with those he sent to follow you. I was obviously wrong, and this means that I've underestimated him twice now. Let me think for a moment."

"What is it about this stuff that makes him want it so bad? Is it some kind of super-concentrated heroin, or something? Rice said he was told that just smelling it would kill him; is it really that potent?"

Ingersoll didn't answer for a moment, but then Sam heard him sigh. "Can Rice hear me?"

"No, just me."

"Good. Mr. Prichard, things are not always as they seem. The product you are carrying is not a drug at all, but a very potent chemical weapon, one that could kill thousands just by spilling it out into the air. It was smuggled into this country by agents of ISIS, through networks that normally transport drugs. The person Rice was taking it to is actually an undercover operative of the US Government who was to take it further to a research lab, to have it reverse engineered for the development of an antitoxin. I can't give you more details than that, but you should be able to figure out who is really behind my operation."

Sam felt his mind begin to reel, and forced himself to keep calm. *Holy Crap, I've gotten mixed up with some crazy CIA thing!* He shook his head.

"What about the guy who's got Indie and the baby? Will he be alone?" Sam asked. "If he is, I can probably take him."

Ingersoll chuckled. "Mr. Prichard, the man you're dealing with was once one of America's most elite soldiers, a navy SEAL, and has spent an amazing amount of time in the employ of the CIA. He's in his sixties now, but as old as he is, I assure you that you could not take him. In fact, I sincerely doubt that any fewer than a half dozen men would be able to take him down, unless they were themselves so highly trained. This is not a man to toy with. Let me make some calls, and I will get back to you in a few minutes."

Sam slammed the phone down into his lap. "Now, look at this crap!" he yelled. "I go out on a limb for you, and now I've got two people I care about who could end up dead!"

Rice looked over at him. "Is it the southern guy?"

Sam nodded. "He's got my—my girlfriend and her daughter," he said, using the official version to save time. "He wants your package or he'll kill them, he says."

Rice slumped down further in his seat. "Man, I'm

sorry. I made a real mess of all this, didn't I?"

Sam shook his head. "I don't know who to blame, Rice, all I know is that those girls mean a lot more to me than you or that damned bottle."

They were on I-70, less than twenty minutes from his house, but the chance that he'd be able to get there and actually save the girls was not good enough for him to risk trying it. As much as he hated the thought of working with an organization like the Company, he didn't see any other way to come out of this with everyone in one piece. He only hoped Ingersoll was not as inept as he seemed where this guy was concerned.

The phone rang and he snatched it up, checking the caller ID to be sure he was answering Ingersoll.

"Go," he said, and Ingersoll began speaking.

"I've asked some specialists to come on board for this operation, Mr. Prichard. I've had your phone tapped, so that when he tells you where to meet, we'll know it as soon as you do. That will allow me to get some people on site quickly, and some of them will have the sole duty of seeing to it that those hostages are not harmed. These are professionals of the highest quality, and will do whatever it takes to accomplish their mission goals. While they are getting into position, however, you will need to go in and do your best to keep him convinced that you are working alone. Do not, I repeat, do not give him the product at any time, for the moment it is in his hands, he has no further use for you or the hostages. If you try to bluff him, he will know it and will kill you. If you try to barter with him, he will lie to you. If by some miracle you get a chance to kill this man, Mr. Prichard, do not hesitate for even a split second, for that is all the time he would need to turn the tables on you, and then you will be the one who will die." He seemed to take a breath, and then went on. "There is hope, Mr. Prichard, but I cannot say there is a lot of hope. The men I've contracted for will do all they can to take him out. If they succeed, be careful, for he may not be working alone. Watch for someone else who may appear and try to get the product, and don't hesitate to shoot if you are sure you have a target! As soon as this is over, call me."

Once again, the line went dead, but this time Sam was ready for it. The line had to stay clear for the old southerner's call, and Sam could only hope that whoever Ingersoll had brought in would be capable of doing the job.

Because he had given the old man a false timetable, Sam decided to keep moving in circles near the middle of the city. That would enable him to get to any meeting place quickly, possibly giving him some advantage. With two innocent lives on the line, Sam was going after any advantage he could get.

The phone rang almost exactly an hour after Sam had last spoken to the southerner, and he answered, praying the old man could not tell the line was tapped.

"I'm here," he said.

"And so am I," said the southerner. "I've been thinking about where to meet up, and I think that we should go to the warehouse. I think you know the one I'm referring to, don't you? The one you visited the other day, before you called Eugene?"

"I know where it is, yes. How do you want to make this trade?"

"I think the simplest way would be inside, don't you? I'll have the loading doors open, and you can drive right on in. When you get inside, you will simply step out of your car, walk twenty paces straight ahead and set the product on the floor, carefully. The lights will go out for a few seconds, and when they come back on, the product and I will be gone, and you will find these two lovely young ladies waiting safely in one of the offices."

"If the lights go out, how do I know they and I won't end up dead? I've got a better idea. I'll go to the warehouse and pull inside. I'll get out, and have the bottle with me, and you send the girls out to me. They get into my car, and then I'll set the bottle down and back out of the building and drive away. When we're gone, you can take that bottle and shove it up your ass, for all I care!"

The line was quiet for a moment. "Mr. Prichard, do you think I've come to the position I'm in by letting people like you dictate to me? If you want these girls to die, then go ahead and try to push me again. I can always track you down and get the bottle after I've disposed of their bodies. Now, once again, we shall do this my way."

Sam shook his head, praying he was doing the right thing. "Nope. For all I know, the girls may be dead already, and you're luring me into a trap. If I don't get the girls, then you'll never get this bottle, because I'll personally destroy it. The only chance you've got to get your hands on it is to do this the way I want."

Indie's voice came on the line. "Sam? Kenzie's asleep on my lap, and he's got a gun pointed at her head right now. Oh, and I fed your stupid dog, Herman! Sam, get me out of this, please?"

Sam made a face. His dog? Herman was the computer program—holy cow, she was saying that there was something on the computer that might help! He spun the wheel and raced toward his house as the southerner came back on the line.

"As you can see, they are alive for now. Test me again, and they won't be. What I will do is this: when you arrive at the warehouse, I will have them in plain sight. You can set the bottle down and walk over to them, I'll leave the lights on until you get there. The lights will go out then, and you will wait one minute, then you may take them and leave, and our business will be concluded."

The line went dead, and the phone rang again less than twenty seconds later.

"You did very well, Mr. Prichard. He expected you

to try to manipulate him, and you played it just right. I've got people moving in on the warehouse right now, and it appears that he is not there yet. If possible, they will take him down before you arrive, but I've given orders to only do so if they can keep the hostages safe."

"Okay, and I'm on something, too. The girl said she fed my dog, but I don't have a dog. That was a code telling me to look at her computer, and that's where I'm going now."

Sam slid to a stop in his own driveway, and hobbled as fast as he could inside the house, with Rice following him. He went to the dining table and opened Indie's laptop. The screen lit up, but at first, all Sam saw was a map of the area. He stared for a moment, and then realized that there was a moving dot, and it had Indie's cell phone number on it.

"Good girl!" he said, and then remembered the phone. "She set her computer to trace her own cell phone, somehow, and that's what he's using to call me. Right now, they're at the corner of Washington and 78th Street in Welby! What the heck is he doing? That's nowhere near the warehouse..."

"The warehouse," Ingersoll said, "is obviously a trap. He's got someone waiting there, I'm sure, to kill you and take the product. He's probably taking the hostages somewhere else to dispose of them, and the only place out that way he could possibly be planning to use would be the recycling center out in Northglenn. I'm diverting forces there now, and they should get there before he does."

Sam looked at the computer. "Okay, I'm going there now. I've got Rice here with me, and I'm parking him on this computer to keep me advised of any changes in their direction. I'll call you back when I know more." This time it was Sam who hung up without a goodbye.

He grabbed Rice and pointed at the computer's screen. "Here's where you get to pay for the mess you made. See that moving dot? You watch that thing, and if it makes any turns at all, you call me at this number." He scribbled his cell number on a piece of paper and shoved it at Rice. "Now, give me that damned bottle!"

Rice handed it over and Sam shoved it into a pocket, then took off out the door, hopping on his good leg and bouncing on the bad one, to make a clumsy sort of running motion. He was back in the Vette and rolling within seconds, heading toward Northglenn at high speed.

He punched the recycling center into his phone's GPS, pushed the big 427 for all it had, and made it to US 87 in only a minute and a half. The traffic at nearly midnight wasn't heavy, and what there was didn't slow him down, but he had a few near misses when he flew through red lights and stop signs. He was in a race against Death, and he didn't plan to lose.

He passed the 84th Avenue exit and suddenly saw police lights come on behind him, but he didn't have time to worry about a speeding ticket. The squad car couldn't even come close to catching the Vette, so he cut off onto Thornton Parkway and took it over to Washington, then turned north again. The police car had kept going on the highway overpass, and Sam remained focused on getting to where he was going. The GPS recalculated after his detour, but he was still only minutes away.

His phone rang, and he answered. "Go!"

"That dot stopped," Rice said. "It's at the corner of Washington and 112th Avenue. It's been there for about half a minute, so I thought I should call."

"Good job," Sam said. "Call me back if it moves again." That was not the location of the recycling center, but it was close. At the speed he was moving, Sam would be there in less than two minutes.

Two minutes can be a lifetime when someone you care about is in danger. Sam shoved the accelerator down as hard as he could, making the old Corvette move even faster as he dialed Ingersoll.

"He's at Washington and 112th in Northglenn," Sam said as soon as he got an answer. "I'm almost there now. Give me something, what can I do to get through this and save those girls?"

"I don't know what to tell you, Mr. Prichard. I've got a team on the way there, but they'll be at least five minutes more. If you can find any way to stall, take it! My team will be there as soon as they can, and they will do all they can to take him down."

"I'll do what I can," Sam said, and cut the call. He saw a sign indicating that the next light was 112th, and began slowing, downshifting to let the engine drag the vehicle's speed lower. At the light, he was down to only forty miles per hour, and managed to turn into a parking lot for a small electronics store. He stopped and let the car idle for a moment, trying to figure out where to go next.

On three sides, the intersection was surrounded by residential areas. Only one corner had some commercial buildings, like the one he was parked at. Farther up the street was a small strip mall, but there were almost no cars in sight. There was no sign of the southerner or of Indie and Kenzie.

His phone rang, and he snatched it out of his lap. It was Indie's number, and the southerner's voice came on instantly.

"Are you confused yet, Mr. Prichard? I see you understood the young lady's message, and found the computer tracing us. Obviously I wanted to get you alone, but I needed to separate you from my former associate, Eugene. Miss Perkins and her daughter are safe and here with me, and as soon as you are ready, we can all meet and get this unpleasant business over with."

"Where are they?" Sam asked, looking around frantically. It was apparent that the southerner knew he was there, and had even wanted him there, but he didn't understand how Indie was involved.

A car across the lot flashed its lights, and Sam eased his clutch out to roll toward it. As he got closer, a door opened and Indie stepped out. Sam sped up and slid to a stop in front of her, then jumped out. His hop-skipping run covered the short space between them as the old man behind the wheel got out of the car and came around to him, dodging a small newspaper delivery van that almost ran him over.

Sam held onto Indie with one hand, and drew his Glock with the other aiming it at the old fellow's face. Indie tried to push the gun down, but Sam held her back.

"Indie, I've got this," he said. "This bastard's been running a game for days, trying to get his hands on a deadly poison, a chemical weapon that could kill a lot of people. Are you hurt? Where's Kenzie?"

"She's in the car, sleeping, and there wasn't really any gun pointed at her, Sam! He told me to say that because he figured the other guys were tapping your phone, by then, and he had to get you away from them. The whole Herman thing was my idea."

Sam looked at the southerner. "Look, I don't know what's going on, but you've got about two minutes before Ingersoll's specialists get here, and they're out to kill you. Wanna start explaining?"

The old man carefully lifted his right hand and showed Sam a card, which he then held out to Indie.

"Show him, please, my dear," he said, and she reached past Sam and took it, then held it closer for Sam to see. It identified the old man as Special Operative Harold Winslow of the Department of Homeland Security.

Sam looked at the old fellow askance. "According to your partner, you're an ex-CIA, ex-Navy SEAL who can't be trusted. Why should I believe this is real?"

"Because if you don't, then all of us are about to die, and that bottle is going to be sold to the highest bidder! I'm trying to prevent that from happening, and I need your help, Mr. Prichard. If you'd let my agents speak with you in Arkansas, we'd be all done with this by now, and my cover would still be intact, but you're an incredibly good investigator. No one else has ever managed to track Eugene down from outside, but you did, and now you've destroyed a fifteen-year-long investigation into channels of entry for terrorist activity! We need to get into a vehicle and out of here, Mr. Prichard, now, before Eugene's team arrives!"

Sam stared at him for a moment, but he knew he had to make a choice as to which of these men to trust. The thing that swayed him was that this man, Winslow, appeared to be completely alone, while Ingersoll was bringing in a team that he referred to as killers.

He looked at both of them and nodded toward Winslow's Lincoln. "Get in," he said, "let's get moving and try to sort this out."

Indie slid back into the back seat with Kenzie, and

Winslow got behind the wheel as Sam got into the front passenger seat. His gun remained pointed at Winslow as the car got moving, but he glanced into the back where Indie and Kenzie were. The little girl was asleep, but Indie smiled at him happily.

"I'm so glad you're okay!" she said. "Mr. Winslow has been filling me in, and he asked me to help him find a way to get you away from the ones you've been talking to. The Herman thing was all I could come up with."

Sam smiled back. "Well, it worked! I saw you had it tracking your phone, and when I realized the phone wasn't where he was saying it should be, I started to figure something was screwy."

"I hate to interrupt the reunion, but do you have any idea where Eugene's men might be coming from?" Winslow asked.

Sam shook his head as he turned back to face the old guy. "No, only that he said they'd be five minutes behind me. I figure we've got maybe two minutes left. Better move fast, and hope we don't pass them on the way."

Winslow grinned. "We won't. Let's make some distance between us, and I'll try to explain as we go."

Sam nodded. "You do that!"

The old man turned south on Washington, then took an immediate right into what should have been the continuation of 112th, but ended suddenly only a hundred yards later. There was, however, a narrow dirt lane that went on through the area, and Winslow followed it. It went all the way to Grant Drive, a thousand feet to the west, and then he turned north onto that street.

"I'm going to tell you a story, Mr. Prichard, one that starts almost twenty-six years ago. Back then, I was still in the Navy, though no longer on active duty with the SEALs; I was more of a liaison officer, working with the CIA on matters that required the special talents the SEALs had to offer, such as recon, intelligence, things like that. Despite the stories you hear, SEALs don't get involved in assassinations and espionage, not usually. My job was to provide special consultants and contractors when needed by the CIA for special operations in other countries." He paused and looked at Sam.

"I'm listening, go on."

"In late June of nineteen eighty-eight, I was approached by my CIA contact about something that they had come across in Iran. There was some evidence of a new terrorist group coming together there, and it's entire purpose for existence seemed to be to destroy the United States of America. It was called Al Qaeda, and there were two men whose names were usually attached to it. Osama Bin Laden, and Abdullah Azzam. I'm sure you recognize those names, they've become rather important parts of American history, after all."

Sam nodded. "Yeah, Nine Eleven, The World Trade Center attack, The Pentagon, etc."

Winslow nodded as well. "Right. Back then, there

was no idea that this group would ever get powerful enough to do such things, but they were getting so much attention that it seemed to warrant someone taking notice. The problem was that nobody wanted to. The CIA had tried to get someone to take on the responsibility of watching these people, but nobody wanted the job, so they finally came to me to see if I could start some fires under someone who might take some sort of action. I was successful in starting that fire, I suppose, because the next thing I knew, I was appointed to be Special Secretary for Intelligence Regarding Al Qaeda, and they became my own personal problem. I reported, at that time, directly to the President of the United States, Bill Clinton."

"How'd that work out for you?" Sam asked sarcastically. "Sorry, never cared for Clinton."

Winslow smiled. "Nor did I, but none of them were any better than any others. All he asked of me was to let him know of any activity by the group that might pose a threat to the USA, and I made my reports daily. I don't think he paid any attention. When he left office in 2001, George Bush wasn't even really concerned about them at all, until Nine Eleven, of course. That day changed everything. Within hours, I was out and the whole department I'd built was handed over to some young kid who was fresh from the CIA's analysis division. There was talk of bringing me up on charges, saying I'd failed to warn the President about the risk of such an attack; I avoided it by threatening to release the electronic files I had amassed over the past three years, showing every report I'd made. Several of them included rumors of attacks on the World Trade Center and attacks using hijacked airliners, not to mention the reports I made about Middle-Eastern flight students who didn't care about learning to land!"

9

Sam smiled. "I heard about that," he said. "You mean it was really true?"

"Yes. Four students from Iran went to a flight school for commercial jets in Florida, and said they didn't need to learn to land, only to control the plane in the air to make it go where they wanted. Most of the staff of the school laughed it off, but one employee managed to make enough of a fuss that I heard about it and interviewed him. That report was one that went to Mr. Bush and was summarily discarded."

"Okay, then where does all this come in? All this going on right now?"

"When I was released from my position, I was then recruited by the CIA, who needed someone to start putting together info on terrorist support groups. They had found that there were many organizations that had a singular purpose: to fund Al Qaeda operations within the US and other countries. Suddenly, I was running a division of the CIA that watched these groups, looked for connections between them and other groups, identified splinter groups that split off from them and built new networks. The damn things grew like wildfires, and most of them used drugs as the vehicle that brought in money. They patterned them after the street gangs we were already dealing with here in our country, and didn't even worry about what our police might do. The war on drugs meant nothing to them, because they paid well to their dealers and pushers and suppliers, and whenever we eliminated one group, two more sprang up to take its place."

"Yeah, the Hydra. Cut off one head, and it grows seven more, or whatever."

Winslow nodded vigorously. "Exactly, Mr. Prichard, the Hydra! No matter how many we took down, there were always more of them! We tried every method we could think of, and finally decided that our only hope was to infiltrate as many of them as we could. I volunteered for that duty myself, and built a new identity with bits and pieces of the histories of other men who'd been involved in the drug trade for a long time, and recruited other older men like myself to help out. We were all placed in different cities, given money to use for capital, and began working our ways into these groups. It's taken me almost ten years to build the cover that I'm blowing tonight, but it's important enough that I'm more than willing to do so. If that formula gets away from us, I don't even want to think about the lives that would be lost!"

Sam's phone rang, but he only looked at it and shook

his head. "Okay, look, I'm gonna admit that I'm so confused I don't know which end is up. According to Ingersoll, you're the bad guy and he's trying to recover this stuff to make sure it goes to Washington to get analyzed for an antidote. Now I've got you telling me how you're the guy who's been fighting terrorism longer than anyone else, and I don't know who Ingersoll is supposed to be! Can you tell me anything that might help me clear this up?"

Winslow sighed. "Eugene Ingersoll was one of my recruits, many years ago. He and I have worked together to build this organization from the ground up, and make it a credible front for terrorist operations. By sheer coincidence, we were contacted four months ago by a member group of ISIS, who wanted to find a way to get a chemical weapon into the US undetected. This weapon, he said, would be capable of killing more people in a single hour than were killed in all of Nine Eleven's events. In the space of an hour, he said, merely pouring the liquid out onto the ground would cause everyone within a quarter mile to die in horrible convulsions. There is no antitoxin known for it, and without access to the formula, there is no way to make one. We agreed to carry it into the country, and I made very special arrangements so that we would not be stopped by customs anywhere, because this is the first sample of it that has ever been revealed. If we can deconstruct it, then it's possible we can make a defense against it; at the very least, we'll know just how dangerous it is, and what it can do. It's even possible that analysis can reveal where it's made, and we could destroy the manufacturing facility before more of it can get out."

"That doesn't answer my question," Sam said. "Which one of you bastards am I supposed to trust now? If you were working together, then why are you on opposite sides now? Which one of you is actually trying to save the world, and which one is trying to destroy it?"

"I'm not trying to save the world, Mr. Prichard, I'm merely trying to save lives. The world, I can promise you, will still be here long after we're gone! Eugene and I are on opposite sides today because he has become disillusioned by the forces in this world that simply don't care, anymore. There are countries right now that would pay enormous sums of money for that bottle, so that they can toss it out of a helicopter over their own capital, or into a region where their enemies are prevalent. I know of one group who would pay well for it in order to use it against Al Qaeda itself, and don't think that wasn't a temptation!" He let out a long sigh. "Unfortunately, Eugene has been offered enough money that he wants to sell, and he justifies it to himself by saying that he has carefully chosen a buyer who won't use it in the US of A. They want to use it in the UK, instead, and it would probably mean the end of the Royal Court in England."

Sam laid the Glock in his lap. "Ingersoll says you're a killer, and that you're the bad guy. He told me he could see to it that this thing gets to DC or wherever, safely, but that if you get it, the girls and I are as good as dead. To be honest, the only reason I haven't tried to kill you yet is because I'm not sure you couldn't take me out before I got it done, but it seems odd to me that if you're as deadly as he says, you'd be talking so much and trying to swing me to your side of this thing."

Indie spoke up from the back seat. "Sam—the thing that made me trust him was that, just before I called you, Mr. Winslow had a gun pointed at my face. When he asked me to get you on the phone, I was about to say no, and suddenly he turned the gun around and handed it to me, butt first, then put my finger on the trigger and pushed the barrel up against his own forehead. He looked at me, and then he whispered 'please,' and I knew I had to help him. Sam, I think we need to trust him."

Sam looked back and stared at her, then turned back to Winslow. He said nothing for a long moment, then took a deep breath.

"Winslow, I'm gonna trust you. I..."

His phone rang again, and this time he winked at Winslow and answered it. "Yeah," he growled, and put the call on speakerphone.

Ingersoll's voice sounded relieved. "Mr. Prichard, you're alive! I've been trying to reach you—what about the hostages? Are they alright?"

"They're fine, at the moment. What happened to your boys, who were supposed to save the day?"

"My men arrived at the intersection and found only

your car, Mr. Prichard, and no one else. Can you tell me what happened? How did you escape?"

Sam shook his head in disgust. "I think you know I didn't escape anything, Ingersoll, because there was nothing to escape. Mr. Winslow and I have been having a very interesting conversation. Would you care to hear about it?"

There was a low chuckle from the other end of the line. "I doubt I'd find it very enlightening, Mr. Prichard, but I'm sure you have. Very well, let's drop all the pretense and get down to business, shall we? We have found Rice, and we have copied the ingenious little program that is tracking Miss Perkins's phone, so we know where you are at this time. I'll give you one chance to turn this into a win-win situation, and then we'll just get to eliminating all of the problems at once. I know you've got the bottle, and you know that I want it. Hand it over to me now, without a fuss, and I'll give you ten million dollars, tax-free. You have fifteen seconds to agree."

Sam laughed. "Fifteen seconds? I don't need fifteen seconds, the answer is *NO!* You stupid son of a bitch, all I want to do right now is get my hands on you! Why don't we do this the old-fashioned way, you and me, settle this *mano e mano*? How about it? You kick my ass, the bottle is yours, I kick your ass, you do life in federal prison! Fair enough?"

Ingersoll laughed again. "Oh, well, I didn't really think you'd go for it. Tell me, Mr. Prichard, do you hear a helicopter overhead? We used your program to piggyback on, and my team is flying up on you right now. I don't think you want to risk the bottle being damaged, so I would suggest you stop the vehicle now, and set it out on the ground. In fact, if you'll do that, I'll tell them not to fire on you, and let you all go on your way."

Sam looked around, ducking his head to look into the night sky in all directions. He glanced at Winslow, and saw that he was grinning. He made a motion as if he were tossing something, and Sam remembered the newspaper van that drove past them as the old man came to talk with Sam.

He'd tossed the phone into the van, knowing that Ingersoll would catch on and start tracing it. That had bought them some extra time, and now Sam had to figure out how to use it.

"Y'know, it's odd, but there are not helicopters around here at all. Are you sure you sent them in the right direction?"

The line was quiet for a moment, and then Ingersoll laughed again. "Winslow, you sly old dog, I have really got to stop underestimating you. It appears you've beaten me, then, doesn't it? If we're chasing the wrong rabbit, then you've got the product and won't make the mistake of being where I can find you again, I'm certain. I'm going to concede this game, then, because I can't see a way to win. Mr. Prichard, it has been a real pleasure, sir. You're an excellent player in your own right, and I hope we'll come up against each other again one day. Goodbye, gentlemen, and ladies, of course!"

The line went dead. Sam looked at Winslow.

"Now what?" he asked, and Winslow laughed loudly.

"We won, Mr. Prichard. We outsmarted him, and within a matter of minutes, there will be no trace of Eugene Ingersoll anywhere to be found."

Sam stared, and in the back seat, he could see Indie staring at Winslow, as well. "You're just gonna let him go? Isn't there any way to catch him? I mean, if I'd known you were just gonna roll over, I'd have called my pals at the PD and they could've picked him up."

"Mr. Prichard, Eugene is not as long out of the trenches as I am, and he's a very dangerous man. I don't think there's much hope we could have caught him, but I can assure you that there will be entire units assigned to finding him by noon tomorrow. He won't get away for long, none of them ever do."

"Oh, yeah?" Sam said. "Then explain Osama Bin Laden! It took more than ten years for your guys to find him!"

Winslow burst out laughing. "Mr. Prichard, don't ever believe anything that comes out of the White House; Bin Laden isn't dead, he's been in a special holding cell under the Pentagon since two thousand and six! He comes in handy, now and then, so we hang onto him! The whole 'Bin Laden Is Dead' thing was so he'd give up any hope of ever being rescued."

Sam leaned back against the headrest and sighed. "You people are all crazy, you know that?" He took the bottle out of his pocket and handed it over to Winslow. "What about this, now? Why on earth was a doofus like Rice trusted to take this to St. Louis, and why was it going there anyway?"

"I sent it to St. Louis because that's where the lab is, the one that was going to analyze it. The lady Rice was supposed to deliver it to wasn't part of the drugspot operation; she's with the Department of Scientific Intelligence. The reason Rice got the job was because we needed to make this seem like a low-priority mission, keep anyone within the organization from figuring out that it had any importance at all. Eugene and I were not the only two deep covers here, but only he and I were privy to the reality of the mission. When I learned that he was talking with a buyer, I called Rice and warned him off, but Eugene managed to send a team after me. That's how I lost my phone and couldn't make contact with Rice again."

"Ingersoll said he told you that I was going after Rice, and that he thought you were following me. I take it the guys who went after us in Arkansas were really his people?"

"Oh, no, they were mine, and if they'd managed to catch you before you ran, we probably could have handled all this a lot more easily. However, now we'll deal with it the best we can. For tonight, I think it best we don't bother to go home, any of us, and we need to get that under secure control."

Sam agreed, and they turned a few minutes later into a residential area. Winslow drove up to a house and the garage door opened, so he pulled inside.

"We're at your house?" Sam asked.

"Not exactly. This is a safe house we use now and then for special operations. Eugene doesn't know about it, and so I thought it would be ideal for tonight. There should be plenty of room, and we make sure there is always food and such. Come on in and make yourselves at home." He climbed out of the car and led the way into the house.

Kenzie had slept through almost all of the excitement, so Indie found a place to put her down for the night and got her shoes and socks off, then lay down beside her and fell asleep, herself. Sam followed Winslow through the house, making sure they were alone and secure, and they put the bottle into a safe that Winslow showed him behind a picture on the wall. Sam admitted to himself that he was glad to be rid of it, and that he was exhausted, so it wasn't long before he was stretched out on a spare bed, his Glock under the pillow.

The first crash woke him, but he heard several more, as people dressed in blacked-out battle gear came through windows, guns in their hands and shouting for everyone to get down and stay down. He rolled off the bed instantly, taking the Glock with him, and looked carefully around to see if he could tell how many he had to deal with.

A shot rang out from a room down the hall, and he heard Indie scream. He was up and moving, his hop-skip helping him hurry along, and when he saw a man in black with a short machine gun swinging around toward his own face, he fired without thinking. The helmeted face suddenly imploded, and blood flew everywhere as the man fell back into the hall. Sam snatched up the Heckler and Koch MP7 almost before it hit the floor, and using it in his right hand and the Glock in his left, began moving in the direction of Kenzie's loud cries.

A motion to his right caught his peripheral vision, and he snapped around to see two men step out of a room. Both were dressed like the one he'd already shot, so he fired the MP7 on full auto, two short bursts of three or four rounds that took both men down at the same time. As he started toward them, he saw Winslow suddenly emerge from the room across the hall and grab one of their weapons, then look at him and motion him on toward Kenzie's terrified sobs.

He turned and started down that hall again as Winslow moved up beside him. They walked low and cautiously to where the hall met the stairwell leading down, and Sam peeked quickly around and down. He turned to Winslow and motioned that there was no one in sight on the stairs, then stepped quickly across and stopped just short of the room where Indie and Kenzie had been sleeping.

He could hear Kenzie crying, and Indie telling her to be quiet, that everything would be okay and Sam would take care of them. He looked quickly into the room and saw that they were on the floor behind the bed. Indie saw him, and started to rise, but he motioned for her to stay put as he turned to the last door on that floor.

Winslow slipped past him and got to it first, leaning his head over to peek in, and then leaning in again and opening fire with his MP7. A muffled curse and a crashing fall from inside told Sam that the old man's aim had been true.

Winslow turned to Sam. "I don't know how they found us, but it's Eugene and his people. They're after the bottle, of course, and we can't let them get it. You understand? We cannot let them get it!"

"I know, and I'm with you. It's downstairs, though, and so are any that are left. Let's get down there and stop 'em!" He leaned around to Indie and tossed her his cell phone. "Call Nine One One," he said, and then he and Winslow were gone. Indie snatched up the phone, but a second later she realized that it had no signal at all, and simply slid back down behind the bed with her daughter and tried not to listen to the shouts and gunshots going on downstairs.

Sam went down first, with Winslow right behind him, and when he got to the landing where the stairs turned to the right, he leaned quickly and checked before moving out onto it. There seemed to be men in the living room area, where the safe was, and he could hear whispering, but couldn't make out what was being said.

Winslow was beside him, then, and pointed two fingers toward the living room and then at his own eyes. He laid his weapon down on the stairs beside Sam and stepped out with his hands wide, then walked slowly toward where the whispers were coming from.

"I'm coming in," he said, "and I am unarmed. Please don't fire on me." He stepped into the room and out of sight, and Sam waited to hear a shot, but thankfully, it didn't come.

"Open the safe," Sam heard, recognizing Ingersoll's voice. "Just open it up and we'll be gone, Harry. No more fighting, no more problems."

"Eugene, you know that's not going to happen. You can kill me if you want to, but that won't get you into it, and no one else has the code. Give it up and leave, while you can. I've had the girl call for help, you know."

"I don't doubt you told her to, but she didn't. I've got a jammer going, there's not a cell phone within a half mile that can get a signal. And you built this place off by itself, so I'm not worried about neighbors hearing us. No, I can stay here as long as it takes to get that safe open. The only thing you might do by opening it for me is make your own life a little easier. It would mean I wouldn't have to kill those poor girls, and Mr. Prichard. Where is Mr. Prichard, incidentally?"

Sam had moved silently down the rest of the steps,

and was standing just outside the door to the living room. He heard his name, and smiled, taking it as a cue, and swung himself around the edge of the doorframe. "I'm right here," he said, taking in the scene in front of him. Ingersoll had to be the tallest of the three men he saw, the one who was facing Winslow, and the other two seemed to be merely waiting for an order. When they saw Sam, they both tried to bring their weapons up to bear on him, but it was too late.

Sam opened fire, taking them both by surprise, while Ingersoll dived for the floor. Winslow rolled himself to his right, putting him on the floor right in front of Ingersoll, and the two men began grappling for the gun Ingersoll was holding. Sam saw one of the two he'd shot trying to get to his feet, and fired once again, dropping him like a brick. He stepped over to Ingersoll and aimed his MP7 at the man's head.

"Give me half a reason," he said, "and I'll be more than happy to pull this trigger!"

Ingersoll froze instantly, and looked up at Sam, while Winslow took his weapon. The old man got slowly to his feet, the gun in his hand also keeping Ingersoll covered as he did so.

"There may be more of them," he said to Sam, "but I doubt it. He would have been counting on the diversion of the men upstairs to throw us off, and probably expected them to take us out in our sleep. Check his pockets for the jammer; he's probably got it on him. Once it's off, we can call in the police."

Sam found it and turned it off, and called up the stairs for Indie to call the cops again, and Winslow called out the address of the house. She shouted down a moment later that they were on the way, but Sam told her to stay put until they had everything cleared.

The police began arriving less than ten minutes later, and it took a lot of explaining and calls to Homeland Security and the FBI to make the locals understand how serious the situation was. Between that and the number of bodies, both dead and wounded, that were scattered around the house, the cops were trying to find someone to arrest who wouldn't be spirited off by the feds as soon as they cuffed him!

That's exactly what happened to Ingersoll. Four special agents from the FBI showed up and took him into custody, making sure he was chained at the wrists, around his waist, between his ankles and then hobbled so he had to walk bent over halfway. Winslow said that would give them a halfway decent chance of not letting him escape, as long as he couldn't find anything to pick a lock with. They loaded him into the back of a van and drove him away.

The interviews and questioning went on until noon, and Sam had to throw a fit to get some food brought in for little Kenzie. When he managed it, the cop in charge had sandwiches brought for the rest of them, as well. Indie thanked him, but the guy was in no mood for politeness, and told her to shut up.

Winslow had told Sam to let him handle the explanations, since there were some things that couldn't be told for security reasons, and Sam was more than happy to agree. The day finally came to a close about three PM, when two men in suits walked in and shook hands with Winslow. Five minutes later, all of the local cops were being escorted out of the house, and Winslow opened the safe and handed the bottle to one of the two suits. It went into a metal briefcase, and Sam thought he'd never been so glad to see the last of something in his entire life.

The adventure, he was told, was over. Somehow, Winslow said the whole thing would come down looking like Ingersoll had tried to make some sort of terrorist deal all on his own, so his cover that he'd worked so hard to maintain would be intact, after all. By the next day, he'd be back to running drug dealers and watching the people who wanted to destroy America.

And Sam could go home and pretend he hadn't helped save the world.

10

Sam got a cab and went to get his Corvette from where he'd abandoned it the night before, only to find that it was gone. He'd left it sitting with the door open and the engine running when he went with Winslow and Indie, and a cop had found it a little while later and decided it must have been the one that outran him an hour before. He'd had it impounded. It took Sam calling in favors from Carlson to get it released, but he finally got home around six that evening. Indie had caught a ride with Winslow, and she and Kenzie were playing in the backyard when he came inside.

He walked out onto his back deck and looked at the two of them, kicking a ball back and forth. Indie spotted him and smiled up at him, then told Kenzie to look who was home. The little girl turned and saw him, then broke into a big smile and ran to him with her arms wide. Sam reached down and caught her, swinging her up and around, and coming to rest with her in a big hug, facing her mother. Kenzie had both arms around his neck, and said, "Sam's home!'"

Sam's eyes went wide, and Indie's went round. They smiled, delighted at the happiness in the child's voice.

Indie stepped up close and patted Kenzie on the shoulder. "You like your Sam, don't you, Sweetie?"

"Yeah, and so do you!" she said, and Indie blushed while Sam laughed.

"Yeah," Indie said, "he's okay, I guess. Think we oughta stick around a while, do you?"

Kenzie nodded emphatically and said, "Yes!"

Sam nodded right along with her, and said, "You just try to get away, just try it! I'm a private eye, baby, I can track you anywhere!"

Indie laughed. "I think I'll take your word for it. Seriously, Sam, this is the best I've felt in a long, long time."

Sam looked into her eyes and smiled. "I can say the same. It's weird, I know we've only known each other a few days, but I'd swear we've been together for months! It's like I just know you, like I've been looking for you, and didn't know how to find you, but I always knew I would."

Indie blushed again, and said, "I know what you mean. C'mon in, let me get dinner started."

Sam, still holding Kenzie, reached out and caught her hand. "Let's go out and have dinner, instead," he said. "My treat."

Indie smiled. "Oh, okay. And is this a date, Mr.

Prichard?"

"It is indeed, Miss Perkins. Is that all right with you?"

"Why, it's fine with me, Mr. Prichard, but you'll need to ask my daughter's permission, of course!"

Sam grinned and looked at Kenzie, there in his arms. "Kenzie," he said, "is it okay with you if I ask your Mommy to be my girlfriend?"

Kenzie beamed. "Mommy! Sam wants you to be his *girlfriend*!" She looked at Sam, and said, "Yeah! That's okay!"

They all went inside to get ready to go out. Sam took a shower, but Indie and Kenzie had already had theirs earlier, so they just changed clothes and Indie took the time to put on makeup and do something with her hair. When Sam came out a half hour later, he let out a low whistle.

"Wow," he said. "You clean up pretty nice, Indie!"

She blushed, admiring the way Sam looked in a suit and tie, and feeling underdressed in her simple jeans and top. "I think I need to go and find something else to wear," she said, but Sam caught her arm and stopped her.

"Why would you want to change when you look perfect the way you are?" he asked.

"Um, because you're wearing a suit, and I feel a little awkward in this getup. I've got a dress. Let me go put it on and..."

Sam stopped her. "I've got a better idea," he said. He took off the jacket and tie and tossed them onto the couch. "Now we can go!" He took her arm and led the way to the van, putting Kenzie in with her car seat first, before holding Indie's door open for her. When they were both in, he went around and got behind the wheel, and drove them to one of his favorite restaurants: Taco Bell!

They ate at one of the outside tables and Kenzie laughed and had a blast. Indie smiled a lot as they ate tacos and burritos, and then began telling him about the furniture she'd bought for Kenzie's room. She promised to show it to him when they got back home.

Sam was spending a lot of time just watching her with Kenzie, and enjoying it. She was a good mother, he thought, and let himself wonder if she would want to have more children. He'd never quite given up on the idea of having a son or daughter of his own, and since he was allowing himself to admit that he was attracted to Indie, he figured he could let himself have a fantasy or two about the family they might have together.

They made it back home around eight, and Indie announced that it was Kenzie's bedtime. This, she explained patiently to the little girl, was part of the benefit of having her own bedroom; it meant she could go to bed at a regular time each night. She didn't bother to explain that the one who got the most benefit from it was the mommy, however!

Kenzie had to show Sam her new bedroom, so he carefully followed her up the stairs and into the room beside the one that had been set up as guest room. He made all the right admiring noises about the beautiful canopy bed and dressers and nightstands and the wonderful Disney playset table and chairs, and the toys that were neatly arranged on the shelves that Indie had bought for them. All in all, Sam told Indie, he had to agree that she'd done quite well with the little bit of money he'd given her to spend, and he was proud of her.

The two adults went down to the living room, and Sam started to sit in his recliner, but changed his mind and took a seat on the couch. He lay back against one end of it with his right leg extended, and just let himself relax for a few moments, eyes closed and head back. He opened them when he felt Indie sit down beside him, and let his leg down so she'd have more room.

"Am I crowding you?" she asked him, and he smiled.

"Not a bit. I'm actually enjoying the feel of someone this close to me; that hasn't happened for a long time."

Indie sat there and looked at him for a long moment. "Me neither," she said. "I—I should tell you that I haven't even tried to have a relationship with anyone since Jared died, so I'm pretty rusty at it. I mean, I know I like you and all, and I want us to—you know, get to know each other—but I'm not in a hurry to go too far, if you can understand that?"

Sam let his hand fall to her shoulder there beside him, and smiled as he caressed it. "I understand, and I agree. I think people rush too many things, and then they regret it. I don't want you or me to have any regrets about us, okay?"

Indie nodded. "Okay."

They turned on the TV and started watching a movie, snuggled together in a lighthearted way. It was just beginning to get interesting when the doorbell rang. Indie said, "Let me get it," and rose from the couch. She peeked out through the window, and then opened the door to Harold Winslow.

"Come in," she said, as Sam got up and walked toward him.

"Winslow," he said. "I didn't expect to be seeing you again anytime soon. What brings you over tonight?"

Winslow smiled and accepted the offer of a seat on the couch. "Sam—may I call you Sam, now, after we've fought side by side?"

Sam laughed. "I'd say that's fine," he answered.

"Sam, as you know, my cover is that I run a drug-dealing street gang setup. Only a few people know the truth, and only you two are privy to it around here. It turns out that I'm going to be needing some help to run it, now that Eugene is gone and discredited, and I wondered if you might be interested?" He held up a hand. "And before you suggest it, I've already given Mr. Rice a promotion, and sent him out to the Vegas operation. That was mostly to get him away from his daughter, but he might know a bit too much for my peace of mind, anyway, so I'm glad he's out of here!"

Sam looked at him for a long moment. "Winslow..."

"Harry, please," the old man said.

"Okay, Harry—I understand that you do what you do for the greater good that comes from being there to spot things like the stuff we just stopped, but underneath it all, the people you run are still dealing drugs. I spent ten years trying to put a stop to that, and I can't see how I could bring myself to work at selling the stuff now."

Winslow smiled. "I thought you'd feel that way, to be honest, so I've got a couple of backup people in mind. The problem is that there will be times when you and I may seem to be on opposite sides, and I don't want to lose the friendship and respect we've acquired. I may need your help at times, doing what you do, and I want to be able to call on you. Likewise, I want you to know that if you need fodder to ease things for you with your friends on the force, I will be more than willing to let you skim off the dross of the organization. Frankly, I hate most of the people who hustle the drugs, and would be delighted to see them get cycled through the jails now and then!"

Sam paused before responding. "I know that what you do is for the greater good, like I said. I can handle that, I just can't handle being down in the mud and mire of it. If you need me, all you gotta do is say so. And you can bet your sweet ass I'll be calling for favors now and then, myself. And as for my friends on the force—I need to give them something within the next day or two. You might want to start hiring, cause I'm gonna dent your employee list."

Winslow nodded and rose. "It's all good, then. I'll leave you be—oh, wait, I just remembered, I have something for you." He reached into a pocket and pulled out a thick envelope. "This is a token of appreciation from your country, Sam. It isn't as much as you deserve, but it's more than the man in the White House gives most people who do so much for their country. I thought you could probably use it."

He handed it to Sam, who opened it and looked inside, then whistled. "I don't think I've ever seen so many hundred-dollar bills," he said. "What is that, about half a million dollars?"

Winslow laughed so hard it scared Indie. "Nowhere near," he said. "I think there's about sixty thousand there, and frankly, the only reason I managed to give you that much is because Eugene had already stolen it and it was off the books. If it were up to Washington, you'd have gotten about a thousand bucks! Enjoy it in good health, and spend some of it on this pretty girl of yours!"

Indie smiled. "I like that idea," she said. "I could use some new clothes, y'know!"

Winslow shook Sam's hand, but when he reached for Indie's, she shoved his hand away and hugged him.

When he finally managed to get free, he smiled and left.

Sam looked at the money in his hand. "I'm thinking that we're going to take some of this and put it away for Miss Kenzie, so that she can go to college someday. Then we'll use some of it to get you an even better computer system, and some things I'll need for PI work, and then we might have to think about a new car for you, cause I'm not sure that Taurus has a lot of life left in it..."

Indie's eyes narrowed. "And just what, I'd like to know, is wrong with my car? I'll have you know that is the one thing I got from Jared, cause he gave it to me when he shipped out for basic, so I'd have it to drive for school. I mean, I know it's not new, but it's paid for!"

Sam smiled. "If it means that much to you, then let's just get it fixed up for you, okay? And I'm sure we'll think of other things around our house we need to spend this money on, don't you think?" Sam suddenly realized that Indie was staring at him. "What? Did I grow a third eye or something?"

Indie smiled. "Do you hear what you're doing? You're saying 'we' and 'us' and you said 'our house' a minute ago. You know, if you're not careful, I'm gonna start to think you like having me around!"

Sam grinned. "Well, of course I like having you around!" he said. "Where else am I gonna find a computer genius who can make me look like a super Private Eye?"

BOOK 2
DEATH SUNG SOFTLY

AVAILABLE ON AMAZON

ABOUT

David Archer was born and raised in Bakersfield, California. He is a fiction author and novelist, writing in the mysteries and thrillers genre. His approach to writing is to hit deep, keep you entertained, and leave you wanting MORE with every turn of the page. He writes mysteries, thrillers, and suspense novels, all of which are primed to get your heart pumping.

The author's books are a mixture of mystery, action, suspense, and humor. If you're looking for a good place to start, take a look at his bestselling Sam Prichard Novels, available now. You can grab copies in eBook, Audio, or Paperback on all major retailers.

Made in the USA
Columbia, SC
11 January 2023